MEET THE GIRL TALK CHARACTERS

Sabrina Wells is petite, with curly auburn hair, sparkling hazel eyes, and a bubbly personality. Sabrina loves magazines, shopping, sleepovers, and most of all, she loves talking to her best friends.

Katie Campbell is a straight-A student and super athlete. With her blond hair, blue eyes, and matching clothes, she's everyone's idea of Little Miss Perfect. But Katie has a few surprises for everyone, including herself!

Randy Zak has just moved to Acorn Falls from New York City, and is she ever cool! With her radical spiked haircut and her hip New York clothes, Randy teaches everyone just how much fun it is to be different.

Allison Cloud is a Native American Indian. Allison's supersmart and really beautiful. But she has one major problem: She's thirteen years old, five foot seven, and still growing!

BEAUTY QUEENS

By L. E. Blair

GIRL TALK® series created by Western Publishing Company, Inc.

Western Publishing Company, Inc., Racine, Wisconsin 53404

Text by Christina Lowenstein

Chapter One

"Hey, Allison," one of my best friends, Randy Zak, called out. "Where do you want these?" she asked, dragging a large biodegradable garbage bag filled with soda cans behind her.

"Take them over to Katie so she can count them," I said.

"What about these newspapers?" asked Sabrina, indicating the piles of paper on the floor.

"Well, first they have to be sorted, and then we can start tying them into bundles," I told her as I pulled a crate of empty bottles across the room. "We have to make sure there's nothing in there but newspapers. That means taking out all the magazines and advertising circulars that are printed on glossy paper."

It was Monday afternoon, and my three best friends, Katie Campbell, Randy Zak, and Sabrina Wells, were helping me with Bradley Junior

High's first recycling drive. There were about six other kids in the gymnasium along with us. We are all members of S.A.F.E., which stands for Student Action for the Environment. It's a environmental club and the recycling drive was our first big project.

I first began to realize that Bradley needed a group like S.A.F.E. after I had helped organize an Earth Alert Fair at school a while ago. The idea of the fair was to make people more aware of the problems threatening the environment, and in some ways it was a big success. A lot of people came, and everyone definitely had a good time. But after it was over, it seemed like a lot of the kids immediately forgot about recycling and conserving energy. I knew there had to be another way to show the kids at Bradley that saving the planet is something we all need to think about every day of the year — not just on Earth day or for an Earth Day Fair.

That's when I started thinking about S.A.F.E., and so far it looked like it might be a pretty popular idea. Quite a few people have joined already, besides my best friends, of course. At the first S.A.F.E. meeting it was decided that our first project would be to set up a monthly recycling drive. That way the whole school could get involved.

The members of S.A.F.E. had gone around Bradley asking the kids and teachers to save their bottles, cans, and newspapers for an entire month. Now, as I glanced around the school gym, it seemed like everyone in the entire school had saved up for a year, rather than a month. I couldn't believe how much stuff we had to recycle.

"Allison, what about these juice cans?" Katie asked, holding up two empty apple juice cans. "Are they okay, or is it only soda cans that can be recycled?"

"Just a minute, Katie, I'll be right over to help you," I called out to her.

I quickly finished counting the empty bottles in the crate in front of me. I added the total and wrote it in a little green notebook that I used for S.A.F.E.'s records. Then I ran over to Katie.

"Juice cans are fine, Katie," I answered. "All aluminum cans are okay."

"All right," said Katie, tossing the cans into the bottom of a large plastic bag and tucking her silky blond hair behind her ears. "Hey, Randy, will you hold the bag open so I can put in the rest of the cans?"

"Sure," said Randy, taking the bag from Katie.

After making sure Katie and Randy were okay, I went to find Sabrina. I found her on the other side of the gym, sitting on the floor surrounded by piles of newspaper. "Sabs, how are you doing with the sorting?" I asked her.

"Phew!" she sighed, wiping her forehead with the back of her hand. "This is a lot of work! And look at my hands!" She held up her hands, which were grimy with newsprint.

"I know," I said sympathetically. I sat down next to her and started to sort though a pile of newspapers. "Next month we'll let people know which parts of the newspaper can't be recycled. If we're lucky, maybe they'll even sort them before they bring them in."

"Definitely a good idea," agreed Sabs, blowing a lock of her curly auburn hair off her forehead.

I looked up and saw Randy approaching us. "Okay, Al, Katie and I have finished counting the cans," said Randy, wiping her hands on her black jeans. "You guys look like you could use some help over here."

"Yes, you could start tying the newspapers

that have already been sorted," I said. "Hey, what was the final count on the cans?"

"Well," said Katie, tying up the last bag of cans and walking over. "We've got 459."

"Wow!" said Randy, looking up from the bundle of newspapers she was tying. "You mean Katie and I counted and bagged 459 cans?"

"Actually, Randy, that's not really as many as it sounds. I mean, think of the number of students here at Bradley." I took out my green notebook and wrote the number down before I forgot.

"Allison's right," said Katie, gathering a bundle of newspapers to be tied. "We should have been able to get more than that after a whole month."

"A lot of people still don't really know about the recycling drive," Sabrina pointed out.

"That's true," said Randy. "Last week I caught Adam Green about to throw his soda can in the regular garbage. It turned out that he hadn't even noticed the recycling bins — which were right in front of him!"

"Well, we'll just have to find a way to let more people know about it," I said. "Maybe that's the next job for S.A.F.E."

"Yeah!" Sabrina said excitedly. "Like a publicity campaign. You know, like the ones movie studios have when they release a new movie or video.

That is one of the things I really love about Sabs. She's very creative.

"That's exactly what I was thinking of, Sabs," I said excitedly. "But I wish there was some way we could get the message to other schools, too."

"You mean, get other schools to start recycling programs?" asked Katie.

"Sure," I said. "After all, the more people that get involved, the bigger difference we can make."

"There," said Randy, tying a knot on a bundle and standing up. "That's the last bundle. What do we do now?"

"I say we head to Fitzie's for some french fries," said sabrina. "I'm starving." Fitzie's is where all the kids from Bradley Junior High hang out after school and on weekends.

"Excellent idea, Sabs!" I said. I realized I was starving, too. "But first let's take this stuff outside and leave it by the back entrance so the trucks from the recycling center can pick it up." I tucked my green notebook into the pocket of my jeans jacket and picked up two bundles of newspapers.

Twenty minutes later we had everything set outside for the recycling trucks. All the kids who were helping with the drive wanted to go to Fitzie's, too, so we made one last check to make sure everything in the gym was put away, and headed to Fitzie's. A couple of kids went on ahead to save some booths, so Sabrina, Katie, Randy, and I got to walk together.

"Thanks a lot for volunteering, you guys," I said, buttoning up my jeans jacket. I pulled my long black ponytail out from under my jacket collar and tossed it over my shoulder.

"No problem, Al," said Randy with a big grin, and stopped to zip up her black leather jacket.

"Al, I didn't mind at all," said Katie. "After all, it's up to all of us to save the environment."

"Yep," said Sabs, looking down at her ink-stained hands and making a face. "But next time I think I'll wear gloves."

We all laughed. I felt just like Sabs. I'd probably have to wash my hands for a week to get the ink off.

"Well, let's hope there will be more than ten

of us doing this the next time around," I pointed out. "If we could get the message across to enough people, sorting and bagging this stuff would go faster."

"That's why we need to come up with a really good publicity campaign," said Sabrina.

"But if we get more people to help, we'll probably end up with even more stuff to recycle," said Katie.

I looked at Katie and laughed. "Hey, that's what we want — more stuff to recycle."

All of a sudden I put my hand in my jacket pocket to make sure I had my notebook, but it wasn't there.

"You guys, I think I dropped my notebook somewhere," I said. "It probably fell out of my pocket at school. I'm going to run back and look for it."

"Do you want us to come with you, Allison?" asked Randy.

"No, go on ahead to Fitzie's," I called, already heading back toward school. I knew that I could run back to school, find the notebook, and be at Fitzie's in no time. "You can order me a chocolate shake!"

I ran back and headed straight for the gym.

But the notebook was nowhere in sight. I decided to check the back entrance where we had stacked the newspapers, bottles, and cans. Maybe it had fallen out while I was bending over a bundle of newspapers.

I looked at the huge stacks of newspaper bundles leaning against the wall. It's amazing how much paper it takes just to print one copy of the *Acorn Falls Gazette*. Somehow it seems like such a waste.

Suddenly I saw my little green notebook lying on the ground between two stacks of newspaper. I moved a few bundles to reach it and stuck it back in my pocket. Then, as I was putting the bundles back, a headline on one of the newspapers caught my eye.

**Local Youth Contest Expanded
to Include Community Service**

Curious, I squatted down to read more.

This year, the winner of the Junior Miss Acorn Falls Pageant will need to have more than just a pretty face. The pageant's promoters have decided to expand the beauty contest to

include an evaluation of each contestant's participation in a worthwhile cause that serves the community. Contestants must be between 12 and 14 years of age. They will be awarded points in the new category of Community Service, as well as the traditional categories of Appearance, Talent, and Academics. The winner will be crowned by this year's Miss America, who hails from Minnesota, will receive a scholarship prize of $1,000, a gift certificate from Dare clothing shop, a local clothing merchant, and a family trip to Disney World. The new Junior Miss Acorn Falls will then go on a speaking tour to represent Acorn Falls at junior high school events all over the state.

Wow, that's really great, I thought. I've always believed that pageants should be about more than just beauty. Maybe the new Junior Miss Acorn Falls would be able to inspire more Minnesota junior high school kids to get involved in projects in their communities.

Suddenly I had a thought. This could be the

perfect way to spread S.A.F.E.'s environmental message. The article had said that the winner of the contest would speak at high schools all over the state. Maybe I should enter the pageant!

I knew I had a pretty good Community Service record, thanks to my work on the Earth Alert Fair and now S.A.F.E., but what about the other categories? I glanced back down at the article in the *Gazette*. Appearance, Talent, and Academics probably wouldn't be a problem — I had always been a pretty good student — but the Appearance category made me feel kind of uneasy. Not that I'm unattractive or anything. In fact, I once modeled for *Belle Magazine*, and I was even given the chance to go to New York and become a professional model. But I'm not really very experienced at putting on make-up and stuff. *Belle Magazine* picked all the clothes for me, and my hair and make-up were done by professional stylists. What if I didn't have what it took to be a contestant in a beauty pageant? And besides, what would I do for the Talent competition?

But then I looked at the newspapers, cans, and bottles stacked all around me. Whoever won this contest was going to travel to schools all over the state. Wasn't that exactly what I had been saying I wanted for S.A.F.E.? Suddenly it seemed a shame not to at least try. After all, what did I have to lose by entering? It might even be fun.

Then I realized that the three people I most wanted to talk to about this were waiting for me with a chocolate shake at this very moment. I quickly tore off a corner of the page with the article, stuffed it into my pocket, and hurried down the street to Fitzie's and my friends.

Chapter Two

"Allison, this is an absolutely incredible opportunity!" Sabrina cried, waving the newspaper article excitedly. "I can't believe I didn't see this in the *Gazette*.

"Ohmygosh," said Sabs, scanning the article. "It says here the deadline for application is Saturday. I don't have much time."

"Are you really thinking of entering a beauty pageant, Sabrina?" asked Katie, popping a french fry into her mouth.

Sabrina looked up at the three of us.

"Well, of course I am!" she said, her hazel eyes sparkling. "Not that I want to be Little Miss Acorn, or whatever it is. But an actress in training has to take advantage of any available chance to perform. Besides, it's great exposure. Sometimes talent scouts go to these things, you know. That's why Allison tore the article out for me. Right, Al?"

13

They all looked at me.

"Actually," I said, clearing my throat, "I was thinking of entering, too."

Sabrina's eyes lit up.

"Oh, Allison, do it!" she said, her auburn curls bouncing. "We'll have so much fun."

"You are?" asked Randy, taking a sip of her all-natural soda and staring at me.

"I was just thinking," I said, picking up the article from the table. "See here, where it says that they're adding a new category in Community Service? Well, the winner of the pageant will speak at junior high schools all over Minnesota. Wouldn't that be the perfect way to pass on S.A.F.E.'s recycling message!"

"That is a really great idea, Allison," said Katie.

"You could become the celebrity spokesperson for S.A.F.E. Every publicity campaign needs a celebrity spokesperson," said Sabrina.

"A shopping trip at Dare and a trip to Disney World wouldn't be too bad, either," joked Randy. "Not to mention the thousand dollars."

"Well, I don't expect to automatically win or anything," I said to Randy. "But it seems worth a try. Besides, it might be fun."

"I'm sure you can win, Allison," said Sabrina excitedly. "After all, how many other girls in Acorn Falls have modeled professionally?"

"Hold on, Sabs," I said, laughing. "I haven't even entered yet. Besides, modeling and entering a pageant are two different things."

"Well, you'll definitely ace the Academics category," said Randy, looking down at the article. She grinned. "I guess all that studying is finally going to pay off after all."

"And of course you have S.A.F.E. and the Earth Alert Fair for the Community Service category," put in Katie.

"Yeah, but I haven't figured out what I would do for the Talent category yet," I said.

"You should sing, Al," said Randy, taking one of Katie's french fries. "You have a really nice voice. And I ought to know, I've sat next to you in music class enough times."

"I don't know . . ." I began, looking from one of my friends to the other. Secretly, I love to sing, but the idea of singing alone on a stage in front of a bunch of people was pretty frightening.

"There's plenty of time to figure that stuff out later," said Sabrina. "Meanwhile, we have to get busy and send in our applications by Saturday.

The article says we'll find out sometime next week whether we've been accepted. Now, we're each supposed to send in a recent photograph."

I looked at Sabrina. "I don't think I have any recent pictures of myself."

"Neither do I, at least not pictures good enough to send in," said Sabrina.

"On top of that, we'd better do it tomorrow after school so we have time to get the film developed before Saturday," I said. Then an idea hit me. "Hey, Randy, do you think you could take a picture of Sabs and me for this contest?"

Randy opened her mouth to say something and then stopped. "I'm sorry, guys, but I can't help you. I have practice with Iron Wombat every afternoon. I begged Troy for hours to let me off his after- noon. We have a big gig coming up."

"Oh," said Sabrina and I at the same time. Then Sabrina got a big grin on her face. "I know, Allison, we can take pictures of each other! We'll use the camera Luke got for Christmas from Grandma Wells."

"Are you sure he'll let you borrow it?" I asked. Luke was one of Sabs's four brothers, and he never seemed eager to do favors for her.

"Don't worry," she said. "I'll get it some-how. When should we take the pictures?"

"How about after school tomorrow?" I suggested.

"Great," said Sabs. "Is it okay if we do them at your house, Allison? That way my brothers won't be around to bug us."

"Sure," I answered. I have a little brother and a baby sister, but things have been pretty calm around my house ever since Mary Birdsong, our live-in baby-sitter, arrived.

"I can't believe this," said Katie, her blue eyes shining. "I'm actually excited for you guys."

"Yeah," added Randy. "I can't wait to cheer you both on at the pageant."

The next day after school, as Sabrina and I walked toward my house, I had to keep stopping and waiting for her to catch up. Not only are my legs about twice as long as hers, but she was also carrying a giant flowered duffel bag that made it pretty hard for her to walk.

"Sabs, what do you have in that thing?" I asked, stopping again to wait for her. "Do you want me to carry it for a while?"

"No, that's okay, Allison," she answered, huffing and puffing a little. "It's just some things I thought we might need for the pictures. You know, clothes and makeup and stuff."

"And the camera?" I asked.

Sabrina nodded.

"But I did have to promise Luke I'd do his chores for a week to get it," she said.

"Oh, Sabs, that's awful," I said, shaking my head. But once Sabrina gets an idea in her head, she usually finds a way to pull it off.

"Here," I said, grabbing hold of one of the handles of the duffel bag so we could carry it between us the rest of the way. "At least let me take one of those straps."

When we got to my house, we walked straight around the back to the private stairway that leads to the terrace of my new bedroom. My old room was right next to my parents' room, so when my baby sister was born, my parents wanted the new baby to have my room. So they built a new room for me as an addition to our house. I've only had the new room a little while, but already it feels like a part of me. In addition to the terrace, there are huge windows on three sides of the room, and because the room is on the second floor, I can see the sky at night when I go to bed.

I put my book bag on my desk chair, and Sabs plopped her duffel bag down on my bed.

"Let's go downstairs before we start," I suggested. "Maybe Nooma made cookies."

Nooma is the name my family calls my grandmother. We are Native American Chippewa Indians, and "Nooma" comes from the Chippewa word for "grandmother." Both of my grandparents live with us, in an apartment attached to the back of our house, directly below my room.

Sure enough, when we got down to the kitchen, my grandmother was just taking a fresh batch of cookies out of the oven.

"Mmmmm, smells good," said Sabrina, sniffing the air. "You make the best cookies in the world, Mrs. Cloud."

"Hi, Nooma," I said, walking over to give her a peck on the cheek. I've always thought that Nooma made better cookies than anyone, and hearing Sabrina say it made me feel kind of proud.

"Sit down, girls, and I'll get you some cold milk to go with these," said my grandmother, motioning toward the kitchen table.

"Where's Mom?" I asked, pulling out a chair.

"She took Barrett to the doctor," said Nooma, bringing over a plate of the hot cookies.

Barrett is my sister. She's just a baby, so she has to go to the doctor for checkups pretty often. When she was born, my parents said I could name her, so I named her after one of my favorite poets, Elizabeth Barrett Browning.

Suddenly my seven-year-old brother, Charlie, came bursting through the back door and into the kitchen. Sometimes I think Charlie would be able to smell freshly baked cookies from a mile away. Mary Birdsong, the college student who lives with us and helps take care of Charlie and Barrett, was close behind him. Mary is Native American Indian, too. In fact, before she came to stay with us, she lived on the Chippewa Reservation where my parents grew up.

"Only take two cookies, Charlie," Mary said to Charlie, patting the top of his head. "Don't spoil your dinner."

"Mary, you've met Sabrina, haven't you?" I asked once Charlie settled down.

"Sure!" said Mary cheerfully. "How are you

doing, Sabrina?"

"Fine, thanks," answered Sabs.

"Stick 'em up, lady, I'm a robber!" said Charlie, pointing his toy gun at Nooma. "Bang bang! Bang bang!"

"Charlie, you put that thing away!" said Nooma, waving a pot holder at him.

"Come on, Charlie," said Mary, taking a handful of cookies. "I've got the loot. Let's get back to our hideout and divide it up before someone calls the cops on us."

"Okay," said Charlie, following Mary out the kitchen door to the backyard.

Sabrina turned to look at me in surprise.

"What's gotten into Charlie?" she asked, ‧amazed. "I've never seen him that cooperative."

"Mary is what's gotten into him. It's like she's got magic powers, at least where Charlie is concerned," I told her.

"Wow, Allison, that's great," said Sabrina.

"You're telling me," I agreed. "Sometimes I *still* can't believe I don't have to baby-sit anymore." I popped the last piece of cookie into my mouth. "Well, are you ready to go upstairs and get started?"

Sabrina nodded, her mouth full of cookie.

We thanked Nooma for the cookies and headed back upstairs to my room.

"Okay," said Sabs, digging around in her duffel bag, "here's the camera. Do you know what you want to wear for the pictures, Allison?"

I shrugged.

"Probably just a nice sweater and some jeans or something," I said.

"Well, I read this article in *Young Chic* that said you should dress to show off your best features when you really want to be noticed," said Sabrina.

"That makes sense," I said, thinking.

"Maybe you should wear something white to show off your dark hair, Allison," suggested Sabrina. "I definitely think your hair is one of your best features."

"That sounds like a good idea," I said, walking over to the bureau against the wall and pulling out my sweater drawer. I didn't usually give my long, black hair that much thought, but it was true that people often complimented me on it.

I pulled on a soft, white angora sweater with a huge cowlneck while Sabrina rummaged around in her duffel bag again.

"Now, *I* figured that I should wear green or blue to bring out my eyes," she said, pulling several pieces of clothing out of the bag. Sabs has really deep hazel eyes, and they become more noticeable when she's wearing green or blue.

"Which one do you like, Allison?" she asked, holding up several dresses.

"Definitely this one," I said, pointing to a long-sleeved, blue-and-green-striped T-shirt dress with a boat neck that I had always liked on her.

After Sabs changed, she pulled a little black-and-white polka-dot pouch out of her duffel-bag. "Okay, now we have to do our makeup," she said. She looked around my room. "Allison, don't you have a mirror in here?"

I shook my head. Except for the new white wicker swing on my terrace, most of my furniture was the same stuff I had had since I was little. When I was younger, I hadn't really needed a mirror for anything. But lately it *had* been sort of frustrating to go all the way down the hall to the bathroom to see how I looked. I decided to ask my mom for a mirror the next time we went shopping.

"I have a hand mirror but it's way too small for what we need to do, so I guess we'll have to use the mirror in the bathroom," said Sabrina, unzipping her polka-dot pouch.

I was glad that Sabs had brought makeup, because I really didn't have too much of my own. We took turns in front of the mirror so we could apply mascara, blush, and lip gloss. I had to admit that when we were finished, I liked the way we both looked.

Next we pulled my bed away from the wall so we could use the wall as a background for the pictures. The wall is painted a really beautiful grayish lavender color that Sabs, Katie, and Randy helped me pick out. Sabs decided that it would be perfect for the photographs today.

First Sabrina took a few pictures of me standing in front of the wall. It was kind of hard to relax and act natural, but I tried. And I wasn't sure whether or not to smile, so I posed with a few different expressions on my face. The problem was, none of them felt real. I was a little worried that forcing myself to smile might look kind of fake. I tried to think of how I had done it when I modeled for *Belle Magazine*.

Suddenly I remembered the photographer from the *Belle* shoot. He was an incredibly energetic man who had kept yelling at the models in Italian. Just thinking about him made me laugh.

"That's great, Allison," said Sabrina, snapping away with the camera. "Whatever it is you're doing, keep doing it!"

Then I remembered that the *Belle* photographs looked natural because the models were all relaxed and having fun.

"Hang on a sec, Sabs," I said. "I have an idea."

I hurried over to my tape deck and popped in a tape that Randy had given me of her rock band, Iron Wombat. She plays the drums for them.

"Great!" said Sabrina as I turned up the volume.

It was even easier to relax with the music blaring. Soon Sabs handed me the camera, and I took some pictures of her posing in front of the wall. After a while we really started getting into it. We each started making our poses sillier and sillier. Soon we had collapsed on the floor by my bed in a fit of laughter.

"Wow," I said, wiping the tears from my eyes and standing up. "It's starting to get dark."

"Yeah," said Sabs, "and we're out of film."

Just then there was a knock at the door.

"Come in!" I called out, tossing the camera onto my bed.

Mary poked her head into the room.

"Hi, gang," she said. "Wow, this place looks like a tornado hit it!"

"Sabrina and I were just working on a project," I explained.

"Well, your mom sent me up to tell you that dinner's ready," said Mary. "Sabrina, you're invited,"

"Thanks," said Sabs. "I'll call my mother and ask."

"When did my mother get home?" I asked.

"She and Barrett have been home for at least an hour!" said Mary. "You mean you didn't hear Barrett crying?"

"I guess we were pretty busy," I said.

But before we could explain, Sabrina and I started giggling again. Sabrina struck another silly pose and soon we were laughing so hard that tears were running down our cheeks.

Chapter Three

"So, how did everything go with you and Sabs the other day?"asked Katie, stirring her yogurt. It was Thursday and I was sitting in the cafeteria with Randy and Katie. We were waiting for Sabrina to show up.

"Yeah," said Randy, popping a grape into her mouth, "when do we get to see the pictures?" She pulled her dark sunglasses out of the pocket of her oversized white T-shirt and struck a fake modeling pose.

"I think Sabrina said we would have them today," I said, unwrapping my sandwich. "At least, I hope so. We have to mail in our applications today."

Katie straightened one of the straps of her pink overalls. As usual, she was completely color-coordinated in her pink-and-blue-striped T-shirt, pink overalls, and blue hair ribbon.

"What else besides pictures do you need to

enter?" she asked.

"We need a transcript of our grades from school, and we have to attach a list of community projects we've been involved in," I explained.

Just then I heard Sabrina's voice from across the cafeteria. I turned and saw her making her way toward our table. She was wearing a long-sleeved yellow T-shirt with a multicolored polka-dot miniskirt, and she was waving a packet over her head with one hand.

"I have them! I have them!" she squealed. Sabs dropped her lunch bag on the table and slid onto the bench next to me.

"And I even waited for you guys before I opened them," she said, triumphantly pointing to the sealed packet of photos.

"Thanks, Sabs," I said. "That was nice of you."

"Okay, so now we're all here," said Randy, pushing her sunglasses up onto her spiked black hair. "Hurry up and open them so we can see them!"

Sabrina tore open the packet and lifted out the stack of photographs.

"Hey, they turned out well!" I said as Sabrina passed me the first few photographs.

I passed them to Katie and Randy.

"These are really good, you guys! I like this one of you, Sabrina," said Randy, pointing out the one where Sabrina was dancing.

"So do I," I said. "That was when I put on the Iron Wombat tape to inspire us."

"Cool," said Randy. "Hey, this one's nice of you, too, Allison." She pointed to the one where I had started thinking of the Italian photographer at *Belle* and was laughing.

"Can I see?" asked Katie eagerly. I handed her the photograph. "Allison, this is really beautiful!"

"Thanks, Katie," I said quietly.

"This is definitely the one," agreed Randy, looking over Katie's shoulder at the picture.

"I guess you're right," I said. "I'll probably send that one in." It *was* the best one of mine in the batch.

"Okay, we know which one Allison's using," said Sabrina, taking it from Katie and setting it aside. "Now we have to pick out one for me."

She spread several of the photographs across the table.

"My pick is that one where you're jamming to the Iron Wombat tune," put in Randy.

"There are a lot of good ones," I said, looking them over. No doubt about it, Sabrina definitely had a certain sparkle in front of the camera.

"Oh, I just can't decide," said Sabs.

Just then I heard the familiar voice of Stacy Hansen nearby. Stacy is the principal's daughter, and she's kind of stuck-up and phony. She never goes anywhere without her three best friends, Eva Malone, B. Z. Latimer, and Laurel Spencer. Our two groups don't really get along, although lately Katie's gotten to know Laurel a little bit, and she says she's not nearly as bad as Eva, B.Z., and Stacy.

"Isn't it unbelievable the way some people just spread their garbage over the lunch tables?" Stacy said in a loud voice, looking down our table, which was covered with photographs.

"Really," agreed Eva with a sneer.

"I mean, hasn't everyone heard my father say that we should all show pride in Bradley by keeping it neat?" she went on.

"Look who's talking about garbage," muttered Randy.

"What was that, Rowena?" asked Stacy in a sickeningly sweet voice. Randy hates being called by her full name, and everybody knows

30

it. Even the teachers call her Randy now. Stacy was definitely trying to bug Randy.

"Listen, Stacy, why don't you just leave us alone," I said quietly.

"Maybe we should go, Stacy," said Laurel, looking uncomfortable.

"Yeah," said Sabrina, two pink spots appearing on her cheeks. "We're trying to do something important here."

"Ha!" said Stacy. "Something important?!" She glanced down at the photos on the table. "I don't see what could be so important about spreading your family pictures all over school property!"

"Maybe they're trading them, like boys trade baseball cards!" cracked Eva.

"Very funny," said Randy. "But we'll see how funny you think it is when someone from this table is the next Junior Miss Acorn Falls!"

Stacy's jaw dropped. For a minute her face turned bright red, and she looked like she was about to explode. Then, just as suddenly, she looked calm again.

"Oh, are you entering that *silly* pageant?" she asked casually, flipping a lock of her blond hair over her shoulder.

"It's not a silly pageant, and yes, Allison and Sabrina are both entering," said Katie quietly.

"I suppose you're going to enter, too, Stacy," said Sabrina with a sigh. We all knew that Stacy couldn't resist any chance for attention, and a beauty pageant seemed like just the kind of thing she wouldn't want to miss.

"As a matter of fact, I'm *not* entering," said Stacy, tossing her head.

"Really?" asked Katie doubtfully.

"Yes, *really*," said Stacy angrily. "Like I said, it's a silly pageant, and I wouldn't enter it for anything in the world!"

Somehow the look on Stacy's face didn't match what she was saying, though.

"In fact," she went on, her face getting redder by the minute, "none of my friends are entering, either. We *all* think it's a silly pageant, don't we?"

"Yeah!" said B.Z.

"Sure," said Laurel, shrugging.

Stacy glared at Eva, who finally nodded.

"As a matter of fact, we have much better things to do than hang around here talking about that dumb pageant, don't we?" said Stacy, looking around at her friends.

"That's right!" said B. Z.

"We *do*?" said Eva.

Stacy shot her a look.

"I mean — *we* do!" said Eva.

"Come on, guys, let's just go," said Laurel quietly.

"You four just better make sure you clean up all this stuff before you leave the cafeteria," hissed Stacy. "Or else I just might have to tell my father that certain Bradley students haven't been picking up after themselves!" She squinted her eyes and gave us a nasty look. "And don't forget — my father listens to absolutely *everything* I tell him!"

"If you're so worried about the trash at Bradley, Stacy, why don't you join S.A.F.E. and help with the recycling program," I said quietly.

Stacy's face grew bright red.

"You think you're so smart, Allison Cloud!" she yelled. "You and your environmental club. I bet you only started S.A.F.E. so it would look good to the pageant judges! Well, don't you forget, there are three other categories you have to compete in, and each of them counts just as much as Community Service! You can't just win by being a Goody-two-shoes!"

With that, she turned and stormed out of the cafeteria, with her clones close behind.

"She certainly knows a lot about the pageant for someone who's not interested in entering," I said.

"That's true," Katie agreed.

"Why *doesn't* Stacy want to enter the pageant?" asked Sabrina. "I was sure she was going to say she was entering and then start bragging about how she was definitely going to win."

"Yeah," said Randy, "that sounds more like her."

"I'm not sure if it's really true that Stacy doesn't want to enter," I said, thinking. "Did you see her face?"

"Yeah," said Sabs, "it was like she was angry about it or something."

Randy started to laugh.

"That was really funny when you invited her to join S.A.F.E., Allison," she said.

"Really," said Sabrina. "Can you imagine Stacy sorting newspapers?"

"No way," said Randy.

"It's funny, though," said Katie. "If you think about it, Allison and Sabrina might not even know about the contest if it weren't for the S.A.F.E. recycling drive."

"Speaking of the pageant," said Sabrina, "which picture am I sending in?"

"I think I agree with Randy," said Katie, picking up the picture of Sabrina dancing. "This one's really good."

"I think so, too, Sabs," I said. "It really shows your personality."

"Okay," said Sabrina, "this one it is."

Just then the bell rang for the end of lunch.

"I've got to go!" said Sabrina, hurriedly gathering up her pictures. "I've got band practice, and I *can't* be late again!"

We all helped her put the pictures away and hurried back toward our lockers.

"Don't forget, Sabs," I said, "you need to get a copy of your grades from the office so you can send it in with your picture today. I'll meet you after school so we can put the applications together and mail them."

"Ohmygosh, I completely forgot about the transcript of my grades!" Sabrina gasped, reaching into the locker she shared with Katie and pulling out her clarinet case. "Thanks so much for reminding me, Allison. What would I do without you?"

"I don't know, Sabrina," I said, shaking my head. "But I know that I never would have been able to enter this pageant without *you*, either."

Chapter Four

The following Thursday afternoon Allison calls Sabrina:

SAM: Hello?

ALLISON: Hi, Sam, this is Allison. Is Sabrina there?

SAM: Hi, Allison. Hold on a second. *(Yelling)* Sabs! SABS!! TELE-PHONE!! Hang on a minute, Allison, she must be up in her room standing in front of the mirror. We can't get her away from it ever since she entered that kooky beauty contest.

(A few minutes later.)

SABRINA: *(Out of breath)* Hello? Allison?

ALLISON: Sabs? I have some news to tell you.

SABRINA: You, too? When did they call you?

ALLISON: About half an hour ago! I was hoping they had called you too!

That's great!

SABRINA: Isn't it exciting? We both got accepted! Now all we have to do is make it through the interview this Saturday, and we'll be in the Junior Miss Acorn Falls pageant together!

ALLISON: I wanted to call you right away and tell you, but I didn't want you to feel bad if you hadn't heard anything.

SABRINA: That's exactly how I felt about calling you!

ALLISON: Did they tell you anything about the interview?

SABRINA: Just that we have to be at the Acorn Falls Convention Center at nine o'clock Saturday morning.

ALLISON: That's what they told me, too. What are you going to wear?

SABRINA: I have no idea. I've been up in my room trying to find something, but I don't have anything that's right. Maybe I'll ask my mother if I can buy something new.

ALLISON: That's a good idea. I'll talk to my parents, too. I guess first I have to tell them about the pageant, though.

SABRINA: You're kidding! You haven't told them yet?

ALLISON: You know how everything that happens in my family turns into a long discussion with everyone involved. I just wanted to make sure that I was actually doing this before we had a big family meeting about it.

SABRINA: I understand. In a way, I wish I could keep this from my family, too. I mean, my mom's been really great, but Sam, Luke, and Mark keep singing "Here she comes, Miss America" every time I walk into the room.

ALLISON: Hey, let's call Randy and Katie and let them know. Sometimes I wish we could all talk on the phone at once.

SABRINA: I know, wouldn't that be cool. I think Katie can do something like that on her stepfather's phone. The trouble is, we're usually all over there at the same time. I think I'll call Katie.

ALLISON: (*Giggling*) Fine, I'll call Randy. If our parents say we can get new clothes, maybe Katie and Randy can come shopping with us for our interview outfits.

SABRINA: Sounds good.

ALLISON: Great. Talk to you later, Sabs.

SABRINA: Bye, Allison!

Sabrina calls Katie.

HOUSE-
KEEPER: Beauvais and Campbell residence.

SABRINA: Hello, may I please speak to Katie?

HOUSE-
KEEPER: One moment, please.

(Katie picks up another extension.)

KATIE: Hello?

SABRINA: Hi, Katie. Well, Allison and I have some great news to tell you. Both of our applications for the pageant were accepted!

KATIE: Oh, that's wonderful, Sabrina! Does that mean you guys are in the pageant?

40

SABRINA: Actually, it only means that we
            made it to the next level. We have
            to go for an interview on Saturday,
            along with the other girls who
            were accepted. But if we pass the
            interview, then we're in the
            pageant.

KATIE: This is so exciting, Sabs. Are you
            nervous?

SABRINA: A little bit, I guess. I wish I knew a
            little bit more, about what they
            were looking for. It would be nice
            to find out something about the
            people who had made it into the
            contest in the past.

KATIE: Well, isn't there some way you can
            research it?

SABRINA: Katie, that's a great idea. I'll go
            down to the library and look up
            information about the pageant win-
            ners of the last few years. They're
            sure to have articles about the for-
            mer Junior Miss Acorn Falls in the
            old copies of the *Acorn Falls Gazette*.

KATIE: That sounds good. That way you'll
            feel more prepared on Saturday.

SABRINA: I'm sure Al will help me. That reminds me, we might go shopping on Friday after school for outfits to wear to the interview. Do you want to come and help us pick something out?

KATIE: Sure, that sounds like fun.

SABRINA: Great. Allison said she'd tell Randy. Well, I guess I'd better go. I have to call Allison and tell her about the library idea.

KATIE: Okay, good-bye, Sabrina — and congratulations!

Allison calls Randy.

RANDY: Hello?

ALLISON: Hi, guess what?

RANDY: Al? Is that you?

ALLISON: Yes, yes, now guess what?

RANDY: Um, I don't know — Mr. Hansen canceled school tomorrow?

ALLISON: No! Sabrina and I were accepted into the pageant!

RANDY: That's great, Al. I knew you guys would make it. Now what happens?

ALLISON: Well, the first thing that will happen is an interview on Saturday. Then, if we make it through that, we will compete in the regular pageant.

RANDY: I'm sure you'll both make it.

ALLISON: I hope so. But first we have to find something to wear. We're going shopping Friday after school, and Katie might come, too. Can you come?

RANDY: Dress for success, huh? Sure, I'll be there.

ALLISON: Great. See you tomorrow in school, Randy.

RANDY: Okay, Al. And by the way, I'm really proud of you and Sabs.

ALLISON: Thanks, Randy. Bye.

Randy calls Katie.

KATIE: Hello. Beauvais and Campbell residence, Katie speaking.

RANDY: Hi, Katie, it's me, Randy. I just hung up from talking to Allison. Did you hear the news.

KATIE: Yeah! Isn't it great! I'm so proud of them both.

RANDY: Me too. I know they're both going to do really well. (*Pause*) Uh, Katie, did you notice anything strange when you were talking to Sabrina?

KATIE: Well, now that you've mentioned it, Sabrina did sound different. She sounded . . . like . . .

RANDY: Allison? Did she sound like Allison? Because Allison sure sounded like Sabrina. After Allison told me about the phone call, the next thing out of her mouth was asking me to go shopping for new clothes.

KATIE: But listen! Sabrina is going to the library to do research on past contests and what the judges might be looking for!

RANDY: Whoa, I'm worried.

KATIE: I'm not.

RANDY: You're not?

KATIE: Nope, I think it's good for both of them.

RANDY: Yeah, I see what you mean. It's good for Sabrina to approach this logically.

KATIE: . . . And it's good for Al to be so excited. I don't think being scared has even entered her mind.

RANDY: I feel like our friend Arizonna. All I can say is, whoa!

KATIE: Yep, well, see ya tomorrow in school Randy.

RANDY: *Ciao*, Katie. Uh, Katie, what if *we* started —

KATIE: Not a chance! *Ciao*, Randy.

RANDY: (*Laughing*) Bye, Katie, see ya tomorrow!

Chapter Five

I hung up the phone from Randy and hurried downstairs. When I got there, my parents, my grandparents, Charlie, and Mary were already at the table. Barrett was napping in her pink baby seat on the sideboard.

"There you are, Allison!" said my mother. "I was afraid the food was going to get cold before you got here."

"Sorry, Mom, I was on the phone," I told her, pulling out my chair next to my grandfather's.

"Must have been a very important call to make you late for spaghetti and meatballs," said Nooma, passing me a plate.

"Actually, it was," I said, pouring myself some milk from the pitcher.

"Hmmm," said my father, shaking out his napkin and putting it in his lap, "sounds mysterious. Are you going to let us in on the secret?"

"Well," I began, "my news is about the

Junior Miss Acorn Falls Pageant."

"Oh, I remember those pageants. They've been having them in Acorn Falls since I was a little girl," said my mother.

"It's a beauty contest," added my grandmother.

"Actually, it's not just a beauty contest anymore," I told them. "This year they've added a new category to the judging — Community Service."

"Well, that's good to hear," said my father. "Maybe it'll show kids that what's inside a person matters just as much as what's on the outside."

"I agree," I said. "Plus, the winner of the pageant gets to travel to junior high schools all over Minnesota to give speeches. It's a great opportunity to get kids all over the state involved in community service projects. So that's why I've decided to enter."

Mary's eyes lit up.

"Really, Allison?" she said. "That's great."

"Sounds terrific except for one thing," said my father. "This sounds like it might take up quite a lot of your time."

"Dad, I really think I can do the pageant

and my school work," I told him. "Besides, I feel like it's my responsibility to give it a try. If I win, I can probably get environmental clubs like S.A.F.E. started at schools all over the state."

"You can't argue with that, Nathan," said my mother, smiling.

"All right, Allison," said my father, "just as long as it doesn't interfere with your school-work."

"Isn't that something!" said my grandfather, beaming. "Our little girl in a beauty contest!"

"Well, I'm not necessarily in it yet," I explained. "I have to go for an interview on Saturday. Sabrina's entering, too. If we make it through the interview, then we become contestants in the pageant."

"How nice that Sabrina decided to enter," said my mother. "That will make it more fun, I'm sure. But aren't you concerned about competing against one of your best friends?"

"It's not really like that," I said. "Sabs isn't entering it just to win. She just thinks it's good experience for her as an actress."

"Well, good," said my mother. "What are you going to wear to the interview?"

"I was going to ask you about that," I said. "I don't know if I really have anything that's right."

"Well, then, we'll have to get you something that's right," said my father.

"Really, Daddy?" I asked. "I can buy a new outfit?"

"Certainly!" boomed my father. "We're not about to send a member of the Cloud family out to do a job without the proper equipment, are we?"

•　　　•　　　•　　　•

The following Friday after school, Randy, Katie, Sabrina, and I all got a ride with Randy's mother to the Widmere Mall. Mrs. Zak said she had to buy art supplies anyway, and there's some big store in Widmere called the Brush and Palette that she likes to go to.

"Okay, gang," Randy's mother said as she dropped us outside the mall, "I'll be back to pick you up in two hours."

"Bye! Thanks, Olivia," we all called as she drove away. Randy's mom likes us to call her by her first name. I'll admit, though, it's taken me a while to get used to doing it.

"Where do you want to go first?" Katie

asked as we walked into the mall.

"How about Giggles? That was where they held the shoot for *Belle Magazine*. I bet they have pageant kind of clothes there," I suggested.

"Great idea," said Sabs, following me onto the escalator.

"Do you guys have any idea what you want to get?" asked Randy, taking off her black leather jacket and slinging it over one shoulder.

"I think we should probably try to look dressed-up but neat," I said. "Nothing too wild or flashy."

"Right," said Sabs, "but we still want to be noticed."

"That sounds easy," joked Randy as we all stepped off the escalator and headed toward Giggles.

Inside the store, it seemed like we looked at hundreds of dresses and skirts. Nothing seemed right. Everything was either too frilly or too casual.

"I really wanted something kind of — sophisticated," I sighed, placing the pink-and-white-polka-dot minidress I had been looking at back on the rack.

Katie held up a hanger with a red-and-black

plaid outfit on it.

"What about something like this, Allison?" she asked. "I think it's a suit."

I took the hanger from Katie and looked at the plaid jacket and matching skirt.

"I might as well try it on," I said, heading for the dressing room.

I stepped into the skirt and slipped on the jacket, examining myself in the dressing room mirror. The skirt was short and pleated, and the jacket fit snugly and was cropped at the waist. It wasn't like anything I had ever had, but somehow I just knew that this outfit would look perfect with a black turtleneck, black tights, and black flats.

"Well, what do you think?" I asked, stepping out of the dressing room so Katie, Sabrina, and Randy could see me.

"Wow!" said Randy.

"Oh, Allison, I love it," said Katie.

"So do I," I said happily. "I think I'm going to get it."

"You should," said Sabrina. "It's perfect. And look what I found." She held up a short emerald-green sweater dress. "Do you like it?"

"Sabs," I said. "It'll look great on you."

Sabs tried on the dress and of course it looked fantastic on her. We paid for our clothes and headed downstairs to the Pizza Palace to get something to eat.

"So, did you guys find out anything interesting at the library the other day?" asked Katie, sprinkling cheese on her slice of pizza.

"Yeah," said Randy, taking a big bite of her sausage-pepperoni slice, "what's the secret to becoming Junior Miss Acorn Falls?"

"Well," I explained, "it's not like there's really any big secret. It seems pretty straightforward."

"Yeah," cracked Sabrina. "You just have to be beautiful, smart, and talented."

"Oh, is that all?" said Randy.

"But that was also before they had the Community Service category," Sabrina pointed out.

"That's true," I said. "So it's probably kind of hard to tell how things will go this year. I guess the most important thing for us to do tomorrow is to try to relax and act confident."

What was weird was up until now I had felt that way. Now I wasn't so sure.

Chapter Six

I could hear my mother honking the car horn below in the driveway as I gave my hair one more quick brushing and slipped on my red head band. There was no time to run down the hall and check in the bathroom mirror again, so I pulled open the back door to my room, stepped out on to my terrace, and hurried down the back steps.

"Don't worry, you look great, sweetheart," said my mother with a smile as I climbed into the front seat of the car and smoothed out the pleats in my red-and-black plaid skirt.

We pulled out of the driveway, and my grandparents came out on the back porch to wave good-bye.

"Good luck!" called Nooma.

"Go get 'em, little girl!" called my grandfather.

Mary was on the front lawn with Barrett in

her arms, watching Charlie ride his bike back and forth in front of the house.

"Bye, Allison!" she called as we drove by. She lifted Barrett's little hand and waved it at us. "Good luck!"

"Bye, Allie!" called Charlie from his bike.

"Well," said my mother happily, "you certainly have some cheering section there. Your father wanted to be here to wish you luck, too, but he had to go out to the reservation early this morning for a meeting."

"I know," I said.

My father is a lawyer, and he does a lot of work for people on the Chippewa Reservation where he grew up.

"He asked me to give you this, though," said my mother, reaching into her purse with one hand and bringing out a little clear plastic box.

I opened the box and looked at the little red rosebud sitting inside.

"Oh, Mom, it's beautiful," I said.

"He thought it might look pretty with that new outfit," my mother said. "I'll pin it on your jacket for you when we get there."

When we pulled into Sabrina's driveway, she was waiting for us outside the house. I was

54

kind of surprised, because Sabs has a tendency to be late.

"Hi, Mrs. Cloud, thanks so much for picking me up," she said as she pulled open the back door and climbed into the car. "Hi, Allison, I'm so glad you got here. I feel like I've been ready for hours!"

"But, Sabs, we're on time," I pointed out.

"I know," said Sabrina. "But I was so excited that I woke up incredibly early, and then, since my outfit was already planned, I was dressed in no time. My brothers kept teasing me about the pageant, though, so I finally decided to go outside and wait for you."

"You look very nice, Sabrina," said my mother. "That's a lovely color on you."

"Thanks, Mrs. Cloud," Sabrina answered.

A few minutes later, we pulled into the driveway of the Acorn Falls Convention Center, the big glass building that's in downtown Acorn Falls.

"Okay, here we are!" my mother said cheerfully. "Here, Allison, let me pin that flower on your jacket."

"Oooh, that's so pretty, Allison," said Sabrina, leaning over the front seat to see.

"Thanks," I answered. "It's from my father."

"That's really sweet," said Sabrina. "My mother gave me her favorite locket to wear for good luck." She showed me the heart-shaped gold, locket hanging around her neck.

"Well, good luck to you both," said my mother, giving me a quick hug. "I'll be back to pick you up later."

Sabrina and I got out of the car and walked into the lobby of the Convention Center. The first thing we saw was a gigantic blue-and-silver banner that said: "Welcome Junior Miss Acorn Falls Pageant Contestants."

Sabrina squeezed my hand, and I felt my stomach jump. I took a deep breath.

"Okay, I guess this is it," I said, heading toward the big double doors below the banner.

We walked into a huge room filled with people. There were several adults walking around and sitting at folding tables, and tons of girls our age everywhere.

"Do you see what I see?" Sabrina asked me in a whisper.

"There must be a fifty girls here," I answered.

"Only fifteen will get to be in the pageant," said Sabrina. "This is going to be tough."

Just then a tall woman with frosted, light brown hair walked briskly over to where we were standing. She was wearing a royal blue suit with a crisp white blouse, and her hair and makeup looked very professional. Even her shoes matched her suit exactly.

"Well, hello there!" she said brightly, revealing a set of perfect white teeth when she smiled. "I see you two haven't gotten your name stickers and your folders yet. I'm Jo Anne Phillips, the contestant coordinator."

She stuck out a hand with five perfectly manicured pink nails on it.

"Hi," I said in what I hoped was a relaxed and confident voice. "I'm Allison Cloud."

"And I'm Sabrina Wells."

"Welcome, Allison and Sabrina," said Jo Anne Phillips, shaking our hands. "Now, if you'll just come with me, I'll get you set up."

We followed her to one of the folding tables, where she looked up our names in a box of files and handed each of us a blue folder.

"In your folders you'll each find a name tag that you should put on," she said. "There will also be a list of three of our five judges, chosen at random. These three judges will interview you and will review the materials that each of you sent us, which are also in the folders."

I opened my folder. Inside was a photograph of me, the copy of my grade transcript from school, and the description I had written of the community service projects I had been involved in — the Earth Alert Fair and S.A.F.E. Clipped to the inside of the folder was a sticker that said: "Hello, my name is Allison Cloud," and a list with three names on it.

"After the interviews," Jo Anne Phillips went on, "we will provide lunch for you while the judges meet to discuss the results of the interviews. After lunch we will announce the names of our fifteen pageant contestants. Any questions?"

Sabrina and I shook our heads.

"All right then," she said cheerfully. "Good luck, girls!"

Her face brightened as she saw another girl walk in the door, and she headed off in that direction.

"Which judges did you get?" I asked Sabrina as I peeled the back off my name tag and patted it onto my jacket.

"I don't know, let me check," she said, opening her folder.

Suddenly I heard a familiar voice right behind us.

"Well, well! It's great to see some of our own Bradley students here after all!" the voice boomed.

Sabrina and I turned around and looked straight into the face of Stacy's father, Mr. Hansen, the principal of Bradley Junior High!

Chapter Seven

"Um, h-hi, Mr. Hansen," I stammered. "What are you doing here?"

"What am I doing here?" Mr. Hansen repeated, chuckling. "Why, I'm one of the judges of the pageant. Didn't my little Stacy tell you?"

"Not exactly," said Sabrina.

"Oh, I guess she was still pretty disappointed about having to be disqualified from the pageant," said Mr. Hansen.

"Disqualified?" I repeated.

"Well, she couldn't very well be a contestant if her own father was one of the judges, could she?" Mr. Hansen asked. "That wouldn't be very fair." He looked around the room. "I am a little surprised that there aren't more girls from Bradley here, though, especially with all those fliers I gave Stacy to hand out."

Sabrina and I looked at each other.

"Fliers?" we both said at once.

"Sure," said Mr. Hansen. "The fliers announcing the pageant. You mean you girls didn't get any? Well, I guess Stacy was pretty busy handing them out, so maybe she didn't get to everyone."

"I guess not," said Sabrina flatly.

"It certainly was generous of her to volunteer to do it, though, especially since she couldn't be in the contest herself," Mr. Hansen went on. "That's why I promised to fill her in on every single detail when I get home tonight. Well, I'd better get to my interviewing table. Good luck, girls!"

Sabrina and I stared at each other as Mr. Hansen walked away.

"Do you believe that?!" asked Sabrina indignantly.

"No wonder Stacy was bad-mouthing the pageant so much," I said. "It was because she *couldn't* be in it!"

"And that stuff about the fliers!" added Sabrina. "Mr. Hansen saying how *generous* Stacy was to offer to hand them out."

"Obviously, she didn't hand any out because she didn't want anyone from Bradley to be in the pageant if she couldn't," I said.

"Oh, no!" wailed Sabrina, opening up her folder and looking inside.

"What is it, Sabs?" I asked.

"Mr. Hansen is one of the three judges who's going to interview me today! It says it right here on my list — 'John Hansen, principal of Bradley Junior High School'!"

"So?" I asked. "What's wrong with that?"

"So, I'll never get to be a contestant in the pageant if Stacy has anything to say about it!" cried Sabrina.

"Hold on, Sabs," I said. "Jo Anne Phillips said that the judges are going to pick the contestants today during lunch. That means that Stacy can't say anything more to her father about us than she has already. And, the way he was treating us, I'd say Mr. Hansen's probably keeping an open mind. As long as you impress him in your interview, you should be okay."

"That's true," Sabrina admitted. "After all, he did wish us luck."

"I'm sure it'll be fine," I reassured her. "In fact, it might even be easier being interviewed by Mr. Hansen, since he already knows who you are." I looked around the room and noticed that lines of girls were beginning to form at the different interview tables. "I guess we'd better get going. What are the names of your other two judges?"

Sabrina looked down at her folder.

"It says here: 'Mike Kinney, former hockey player for the Minnesota Wingers,' and 'Lisa Lazure, D.J. on radio station WKZAP,"' she read.

"I have Lisa Lazure, too," I said, looking down at my list. "My other two are 'Roberta Andrews, advertising executive for Limelight Cosmetics' and 'Arthur Lawrence, owner of Dare clothing stores.'"

"Oooh, you're so lucky, Allison," said Sabrina. "Dare is my favorite store!"

"Let's get on line for Lisa Lazure first, since she's the only one we both have," I suggested, looking around.

"Okay," Sabrina agreed. "Hmmm, Lisa Lazure. I think I've heard of her."

"That must be her over there," I said, pointing toward the table I had spotted with Lisa Lazure's nameplate on it. Behind the table sat a small, dark-haired young woman in a black turtleneck. "We'll have to ask Randy about her," I said, heading toward the line. "She knows all the D.J.s on WKZAP."

As we waited on line with our folders, I looked around at the other girls. A few who were wearing pants looked a little too casual, and one girl had on a puffy pink dress that looked like it would be better for a prom, but most of the girls were dressed well. I glanced down at my red-and-black plaid suit and decided that I had definitely chosen the right outfit. And the rosebud from my father on the jacket was the perfect finishing touch.

As we moved closer to the head of the line, I felt a nervous feeling start in my stomach. I tried to take deep breaths and relax, but it was still there when I had reached the head of the line.

I heard Sabrina whisper, "Good luck!" as I approached the table and sat in the empty chair.

"Welcome," Lisa Lazure said, taking my folder and flipping it open. Her voice was deep and breathy at the same time, and I could see why she had a job on the radio. "Allison Cloud, what a wonderful name. It almost sounds like a D.J. tag name."

"Thank you," I said. "Actually, Cloud is a Native American name. I'm a Chippewa Indian."

"Really! Well, it's a great name if you ever want to get into radio," she said, looking over the information in my folder. "It says here that you founded an environmental club at your school, Allison. Why don't you tell me about it?"

I explained how the idea for S.A.F.E. had come to me after the Earth Alert Fair, how we were concentrating on recycling at first, and how I hoped to spread the message and get clubs like S.A.F.E. started at other schools, too.

"Actually," I added, "that's one of the main reasons I want to enter the pageant. Whoever becomes Junior Miss Acorn Falls will have an excellent opportunity to communicate with other junior high school students."

"That's very admirable, Allison," said Lisa Lazure in her silky-sounding voice. "I've always believed that those of us who have the chance to reach a lot of people also have a responsibility to spread important messages. That's why I've always tried to use my radio program as a way to educate people about the problems facing our world today."

She asked me a few more questions about S.A.F.E., school, and my family, and then the interview was over. I stood up, thanked her, and winked quickly at Sabrina as she took my place in the interview chair.

It seemed like it had gone pretty well, but it was hard to tell. Lisa Lazure was definitely easy to talk to, though, and that made me feel a little more confident about the next two interviews.

I decided to go see Roberta Andrews, the advertising executive for Limelight Cosmetics, next.

Roberta Andrews turned out to be a pretty woman with short strawberry-blond hair and lots of gold jewelry. As I took my seat across the table from her, I could smell her perfume.

The first thing she asked me was if I had ever modeled. She didn't seem surprised when I explained that I had done a little bit for *Belle*, but she wondered why I hadn't gone on to do more.

"Well, I had the chance to," I said. "But it would have meant leaving Acorn Falls and going to live in New York, and I didn't think I was ready to make that kind of a change yet."

She never even mentioned S.A.F.E. or the Earth Alert Fair, but she did ask me how tall I was and what I weighed.

A few minutes later, the interview was over and I was on my way to see the third judge, Arthur Lawrence, the owner of Dare clothing stores.

Mr. Lawrence, a heavy set black man in a business suit, seemed especially interested in my school record. He kept looking over the transcript of my grades and asking me questions about my classes.

Then he asked me what I thought I might want to be when I grew up. I told him I wasn't sure yet, but that sometimes I thought about becoming a writer.

"Oh, really?" he said, his eyes lighting up. "And who are some of your favorite writers?"

"Well, I love Elizabeth Barrett Browning's poetry," I told him. "And I just finished reading Shakespeare's *Romeo and Juliet.*"

He smiled.

"Thank you very much, Allison," he said, shaking my hand.

Jo Anne Phillips was announcing that lunch was being served in the next room, so I looked around for Sabrina. I finally saw her sitting across the table from Mike Kinney, the former hockey player. Sabs was talking excitedly, waving her hands around, and Mike Kinney, who was heavy set and had a blond crew cut, was giving her a huge smile.

Suddenly I heard a voice next to me.

"Are you going into lunch?" the voice asked quietly.

I turned to see a tall, thin black girl standing by my side. She had huge, almond-shaped brown eyes and very high cheekbones. She was wearing a bright pink minidress with a matching cropped jacket, and she almost looked like she could have been a model.

"Actually, I'm waiting for my friend to finish her interview," I said, indicating Sabrina, who was still deep in conversation with Mike Kinney.

"She looks like she's doing really well," the girl said. "I wish I could feel that comfortable being interviewed."

"I know," I said, smiling. "Me too. Sabs is just like that. She can talk to anybody. By the way, my name's Allison. Allison Cloud."

"I'm Jeanine Jones," the girl said.

"Here comes Sabrina," I said, seeing Sabrina stand up from the table and shake Mike Kinney's hand. "Why don't we all go in and eat together?"

"That would be great," said Jeanine. "I don't really know anyone here."

Just then Sabrina arrived. Her hazel eyes were sparkling and her cheeks were very pink.

"Wow!" she said excitedly. "This is so much fun! I just love meeting new people."

"I wish I felt that way," said Jeanine. "The interview's not exactly my favorite part of all this."

I introduced Sabrina to Jeanine, and the three of us headed into the next room, where we helped ourselves to some food from the buffet and sat down at an empty table.

"Mmmm, great food," said Sabrina, digging into her potato salad.

"I wish I felt like eating," said Jeanine. "I'm still kind of nervous."

Then a pretty girl with long, wavy brown hair, and wearing a white blouse and a flared red skirt, walked over to our table.

"Is anybody sitting here?" asked, putting her plate down on the table near an empty chair.

"No, go right ahead," I answered.

"Hi," said Sabrina, popping open her can of soda. "I'm Sabrina Wells. And this is Allison

Cloud and Jeanine Jones."

"I'm Marcy Burroughs," said the girl, pulling out her chair and sitting down. "So, how did everything go for all of you this morning?"

"I think I did all right," I started. "It's hard to tell, though —"

But just then I was cut off by a girl with shoulder-length, wavy blond hair who walked up to our table. She was wearing a pale blue-and-white flowered dress with a puffy skirt, and the blue of her dress matched her eyes exactly.

"Whew!" she sighed, putting her plate of food down on our table and flopping into an empty chair. "Some morning, huh? Hi, everyone, I'm Veronica Lane Callahan. But you can all call me Nicki. That's my nickname. Don't ask me how I got it, but everyone calls me Nicki," she said, giving us all a wink.

"Hi, Nicki, I'm Allison," I said. "As a matter of fact, Sabrina, Jeanine, Marcy, and I were all just talking about how it went this morning."

"Well, I'd say it was pretty routine," Nicki began.

"Routine?" Sabrina asked. "You mean you've done this before?"

"Have I ever!" said Nicki, rolling her eyes. "This is my fifth pageant. After a while you get to learn the ropes. They all ask the same questions: 'What do you want to be when you grow up?' — 'What are your favorite books?' You learn what to say."

"Have you really been in five pageants?" I asked her.

"Sure have," she answered. "Counting this one, that is. Let's see, there was the Junior Miss Lake Superior Pageant, the Junior Miss Alfa Hair Care Products Pageant, the Junior Miss North Star State Pageant, and the Junior Miss Swedish-American Pageant — I won that one."

"Really?" asked Sabrina. "Are you Swedish-American?"

"Well, one of my grandmothers is," said Nicki. "But that's all I needed to enter!"

"So what do you think of this pageant so far?" asked Jeanine. "I mean, since you've had experience with them before."

Nicki wrinkled her nose and thought a moment.

"Pretty run-of-the-mill, I'd say," she

answered. "Except for that new stuff about Community Service. Now, *that* could really throw you for a loop if you weren't prepared."

"No kidding," said Marcy. "I haven't really done anything like that. I didn't know what to say when they asked me about it."

"Believe me," said Nicki. "It's not even really how much you do so much as *how* you present yourself. Take me, for example. I volunteer at three different charities."

"Really, *three*?" I said.

"How do you find the time?" Jeanine wanted to know.

"Actually, it doesn't really take up any more time than if I just volunteered at one, because I alternate," Nicki explained. "But it sure looks a lot better to the judges."

"It seems like you'd be able to accomplish a lot more if you just stuck with one thing, though," said Jeanine. "For example, I volunteer at a program to help tutor little kids. If I didn't show up every week to help out, the kids I'm working with might never make any progress."

"Oh, you're probably right." Nicki shrugged. "But try explaining *that* to the judges."

Suddenly Jo Anne Phillips appeared at the front of the room and clapped her hands for attention.

"Ladies, the time has come for the big announcement," she said. "If you'll just file back into the other room, the judges have decided who our fifteen contestants will be."

A murmur went through the crowd of girls.

"Ooooh, I love this part," said Nicki excitedly. "Good luck, everyone."

"Come on, Sabs," I said, grabbing her hand and following the crowd into the next room. "This is it!"

We settled ourselves into the folding chairs that had been set up while we were eating. Jo Anne Phillips stood in front of us, waiting for the crowd to quiet down, while the judges sat behind her in their own row of chairs.

"First of all," Jo Anne Phillips began, "I would like to thank each and every one of you for coming down here today. I know I speak on behalf of our judges when I say that this is a very difficult choice to make."

"I wish she would just get to the point," Sabrina whispered.

"I am going to ask that those girls whose

names I read come up here and stand next to me," Jo Anne Phillips continued. "I will then give you your official Junior Miss Acorn Falls Pageant sash to put on. You will be required to wear your sashes all of our rehearsals, as well as at the pageant. I'd like to ask the rest of you to please hold your applause and cheers until all fifteen names have been read."

She took a slip of paper out of the pocket of her blue suit and cleared her throat. I felt Sabrina's hand tighten in mine.

"Contestant Number 1 — Jeanine Jones."

I watched as Jeanine jumped up and hurried to the front of the room. Jo Anne Phillips handed her a white sash with "JMAF — Contestant #1" printed on it, and Jeanine draped it over one shoulder and across her chest to the opposite hip.

"Contestant Number 2 — Elizabeth Lee."

A tall Asian-American girl with shoulder-length black hair stood up and hurried to the front of the room to get her sash.

Jo Anne Phillips continued to read from the list, and several more girls went up to receive their sashes.

Suddenly I heard her say, "Contestant

Number 8 — Sabrina Wells."

I was so excited, I almost forgot what Jo Anne Phillips had said about saving our applause and cheers for the end. I gave Sabs a quick hug and watched as she nearly flew to the front of the room.

I didn't take my eyes off Sabrina after that. She looked so happy, standing up there with her "JMAF — Contestant #8" sash on. But as the list went on, and the line of girls in sashes became longer, I began to worry that I wasn't going to make it.

By the time Jo Anne Phillips read, "Contestant Number 11 — Veronica Lane Callahan," and I watched Nicki bounce up to the front of the room, my whole body was starting to feel numb.

But then I heard it: "Contestant Number 12 — Allison Cloud."

I made my way through the rows of folding chairs as fast as I could. When I was almost at the front, I felt a little tap on my arm.

It was Marcy Burroughs, the girl from the lunch table.

"Congratulations," she whispered.

I barely had time to thank Marcy before I felt Sabrina's arms around me.

"We made it! We made it!" Sabrina yelled, trying to jump up and down and hug me at the same time.

I was barely aware of Jo Anne Phillips reading the last of the names as Sabs threw my sash over my head and helped me position it across my body.

To the sound of the loud applause of the rest of the girls, I straightened out my sash and proudly took my place in line as Contestant Number 12 of the Junior Miss Acorn Falls Pageant.

Chapter Eight

After Sabrina and I had told her the great news, I asked my mother to drop us off at Fitzie's. Katie and Randy had promised to wait for us there, and I knew they must be anxious to hear what had happened at the Convention Center.

Sabs and I practically burst in the door and over to our usual table. We both still had our pageant sashes on, so the minute Katie and Randy saw us, they knew we had made it. They both jumped up from the table and threw their arms around us in one great big hug.

"All right!" yelled Randy happily. "This calls for ice cream sundaes all around!"

"Really," agreed Katie. "Our treat, right, Randy?"

"Sure thing," said Randy. "I'll go order them. But then you two have to tell us every detail."

Randy walked up to the counter and

returned with a tray of four of the biggest ice cream sundaes I had ever seen.

"Okay," she said. "Four with the works. Now tell us what happened today."

"Really," said Katie, digging into her sundae. "I'm so excited."

"Well, first of all, there were tons of girls there," I told them. "Sabs and I were pretty worried, since we knew they could only pick fifteen of us."

"No problem," scoffed Randy. "Those judges obviously had good taste."

"That's another thing," said Sabrina. "You'll never guess who one of the judges turned out to be — Mr. Hansen!"

"You're kidding," said Katie.

"No, really," I said. "It turns out that that's why Stacy was bad-mouthing the pageant so much — she did want to enter, but she was disqualified because her father is one of the judges!"

"Not only that," Sabrina added. "But Stacy was supposed to pass out fliers about the pageant to all the girls in school."

"I get it," said Randy. "She didn't want anyone else to enter if she couldn't, so she passed out the fliers to all the garbage cans in school instead."

"Right, only Mr. Hansen doesn't know that," I said. "You should have heard him talking about how generous it was of his little Stacy to help out like that!"

"Wait a minute," said Katie. "Remember all that stuff Stacy said about telling her father on us if we didn't clean up at lunch that day? She kept saying that her father listens to *everything* she tells him. Do you think she might try to talk Mr. Hansen into giving you guys low scores in the pageant?"

"I'm sure she's tried already," I said. "She knows we're in the contest but obviously it hasn't worked. I mean, we got this far, didn't we?"

"Besides," added Sabrina. "Mr. Hansen was one of the judges who interviewed me, and he was really nice to me."

"What about the other judges?" asked Katie. "What were they like?"

"One of them was a D.J. from WKZAP," I said. "We thought you might know who she is, Randy. Her name is Lisa Lazure."

"Sure!" said Randy, brightening. "Lisa Lazure — the Night Owl."

"Huh?" said Katie.

"Lisa Lazure does this mellow radio show Thursday through Saturday nights. It's on late, though. She calls herself the Night Owl," Randy explained.

"No wonder her name sounded so familiar," said Sabrina.

"So, tell us about the other contestants," said Katie.

"Well," I said, "we met this really nice girl named Jeanine."

"And this really unbelievable one named Nicki," added Sabrina. "She's already been in four other pageants, and she even won one of them. It was almost like she was a professional pageant contestant!"

We all laughed.

"She did seem very sure of herself," I agreed.

"So, what's next for you guys?" asked Randy.

"Well, we have rehearsals for the next two weeks," I explained.

"And we're each supposed to have to get a solid-color, one-piece bathing suit and an evening gown," said Sabrina.

"Have you decided what you're doing for

the Talent competition?" Katie wanted to know.

"Methinks I have an idea," said Sabs.

"Sabrina! Don't tell me you're going to play Juliet?" I said, laughing.

"That's a great idea!" said Katie.

"But what are you going to do about Romeo?" I asked. "Everything in the Talent competition has to be performed alone."

"Leave it to me," said Sabs, her eyes twinkling mischievously. "I think I may have a solution."

"What about you, Allison?" asked Katie. "Have you decided what you're going to do?"

"Al's going to sing!" said Randy. "Right?"

"I don't know, Randy . . ." I began.

"Oh, come on!" said Randy. "I told you — you've got a great voice. All you need to do is pick a song you really like."

"Well, I'll think about it," I said. I just wish it weren't so hard to imagine myself singing in front of strangers.

•   •   •   •

The first pageant rehearsal was on Monday after school. Sabrina and I sat with the other thirteen contestants at the Convention Center listening to Jo Anne Phillips.

We were in the same room we had been in on Saturday, but now it looked completely different. The folding tables were gone, and a wooden platform, like a stage, had been erected at one end of the huge room. Pushed up against the side of the stage was a grand piano. There were workers all over the place, hammering and sawing, and a man on a giant ladder was hanging a big, blue, velvet curtain against the wall behind the stage.

I was wearing my pageant sash over an oversized white T-shirt and a pair of purple-and-white-flowered leggings. Sabs looked cute with her pageant sash over a pale gray turtleneck and black cropped jeans.

Jo Anne Phillips had on a salmon-pink suit almost exactly like the blue one she had been wearing on Saturday. As before, her shoes matched her suit perfectly, and every hair was in place.

"Now, ladies," she was saying, "from now on I'd like you to bring the shoes you will be wearing for the pageant with you so that you can practice walking on the stage with them. We don't want anyone to stumble during the pageant!"

Nicki raised her hand.

"I brought my shoes with me today, Miss Phillips," she said, holding up a little white tote bag.

Jo Anne Phillips smiled, showing us her perfect white teeth.

"What good thinking," she said, beaming at Nicki. "Now, ladies, I'd like to introduce our pageant choreographer, Mr. John Deegan."

She beckoned across the room to a thin but well-built blond man who was up on the stage talking to one of the workers. The man jumped gracefully down from the stage and walked over to where we were all sitting.

As he got closer, a few of the contestants began to murmur, and I could see why. John Deegan was very good-looking, with his slicked-back blond hair and his sparkling blue eyes.

Sabrina jabbed me in the ribs with her elbow.

"He's cute," she whispered.

"Hi, there, folks," John Deegan said with a smile. "Today I'm going to be teaching you the opening dance number for the show. Now, don't worry if you've never had any dance training before — there will be a part for everyone in this. I'd like to start out with a few basic stretches, so if you would all just stand up and make sure you have enough space around you, we'll begin."

For the next ten minutes, as John Deegan led us through a series of stretching exercises, I began to be really happy that I had decided to wear comfortable clothes to this rehearsal.

After we had finished warming up, he began to teach us the dance steps. I wasn't really used to so much exercise, and I was glad my part turned out to be pretty small. Sabrina looked like she was having a ball, though, and her face lit up when John Deegan gave her an extra series of steps to do on her own.

The real stars of the routine turned out to be Jeanine and Nicki, though. Jeanine had been taking ballet since she was really little, and all of her movements were incredibly graceful. John Deegan gave her a solo part in the dance almost immediately.

Nicki seemed to have studied every kind of dance there was. She claimed to have taken jazz, ballet, tap, and even belly dancing — although after what she had told us about the three different charities she worked for, I couldn't help wondering how much time she had actually spent studying all these dance styles. She definitely had a real stage presence, though. Maybe it was because she never seemed to doubt what she was doing. I wasn't too surprised when John Deegan gave her a solo part, too.

When it seemed like we had run through the routine a hundred times, John Deegan finally gave us a break.

I flopped into a chair and took a deep breath. Even Sabrina, who was always so energetic, was sitting in the chair next to me, looked exhausted. Everyone was relieved when Jo Anne Phillips came around with a tray of bottles of juice.

But our break lasted only a few minutes. Next we were introduced to Mrs. White, the chubby, white-haired woman who was going to be our music coach.

"All right, girls," Mrs. White said in a high, trembly-sounding voice. "I'd like you each to take a copy of the lyrics that are on the piano, and then assemble in a row on the stage, please."

I stood in line to get one of the printed pages from the piano and climbed up the steps to the stage.

I stood in my place between Contestant Number 11, Nicki Callahan, and Contestant Number 13, a tall blond girl I hadn't met yet.

"Hi," I whispered to Contestant Number 13, as Mrs. White took her seat behind the piano. "I'm Allison Cloud."

"I'm Christie French," she said, smiling. "Nice to meet you."

Just then Mrs. White struck two loud, deep chords on the piano, and we all snapped to attention.

"We will now go through the song," said Mrs. White. "And we will continue to go through it until everyone has it right. You may use your lyric sheets today, but I expect everyone to have this memorized by the next rehearsal. Does everyone understand?"

We all nodded.

I looked down at the sheet in front of me. The song was called "Sing! Sing! Sing!" It was pretty simple, and I didn't think it would be too hard to learn.

Mrs. White began playing, and we all started to sing. At first no one was very sure of the melody, so we all sang kind of softly. By the second verse, though, I felt like I knew what I was doing, and I began to sing a little louder. Christie French, who was next to me, raised her voice, too, and I could hear that she sang very well. Before long the rest of the girls were singing more strongly.

After we had gone through the song a few times, Mrs. White asked us each to sing a couple of lines on our own.

Jeanine Jones went first, but her voice was so soft you could barely hear it.

Next came Elizabeth Lee, the Asian-American girl with the shoulder-length black hair. Her voice was but strong and as clear as a bell.

A few more of the girls went, including Sabrina and Nicki, who did pretty well, too. Then it was my turn. I took a deep breath, relaxed, and sang my two lines. Next came Christie, who sounded as good as I expected. I was surprised to hear that Contestant Number 14, a pale girl with very dark hair, could hardly carry a tune at all.

When we had finished singing our lines, Mrs. White made an announcement.

"From now on, everyone will sing the chorus together as before, but I am assigning the three verses as solos," she told us. "The first verse will be sung by Contestant Number 13."

I looked at Christie French, who was beaming.

"Contestant Number 2 will sing verse two," Mrs. White went on. I knew that was Elizabeth Lee. "And verse three will be sung by Contestant Number 12."

It took me a moment to realize that she meant me. Then I saw Sabrina smiling at me from her spot in the line. All of a sudden I realized what had happened: Mrs. White had picked me for a solo! I felt really proud. I have to admit, I was a little bit nervous, too, but mostly I was just excited about it.

. "All right, girls, end of rehearsal," said Mrs. White, closing the lid of the piano. "Make sure you all have your parts memorized for next time, especially you soloists. I don't want to see those lyrics in anyone's hands anymore."

As we were gathering our things to leave, Jo Anne Phillips stopped us so she could make one last announcement.

"We're going to have to start organizing the Talent competition," she said. "Now, how many of you plan to play an instrument?"

Two girls raised their hands.

"And how many plan to sing?"

I hardly had time to think before I raised my hand. I was still a little nervous about singing in front of an audience. But hadn't Mrs. White singled me out for a solo in the song? She wouldn't have done that if she hadn't believed I could do it, would she? As Randy had said, now all I had to do was find a song I really liked.

Jo Anne Phillips took a count of what the other girls planned to do, and told those of us who were singing to bring our music to Mrs. White by next Monday's rehearsal.

I took a deep breath. That meant I had exactly a week to find a song I really liked.

Chapter Nine

"Oh, Allison, this is such fun," my mother said, fingering the rack of long dresses in front of her. "You and I should really go shopping together more often."

It was Thursday after school, a week and two days before the pageant, and my mother and I were looking for a gown for me at Flights of Fancy, the formal shop on Main Street.

"May I help you with something?" asked the saleswoman, walking over to us.

"Yes," my mother answered, "we're looking for a formal gown."

"And what sort of occasion might this be for?" asked the saleswoman, looking at me. "A first formal dance, perhaps?"

"Actually, it's a pageant," I explained. "The Junior Miss Acorn Falls Pageant."

"Oh, yes, of course," said the saleswoman. "We've supplied gowns for that pageant for many years. Are you a contestant, miss?"

"Yes, she is," said my mother proudly.

"Well, then, we'll have to find you a very special gown," said the saleswoman, looking through one of the racks and starting to pull out dresses for me to see.

Twenty minutes later I had picked out three that I really liked. The first one I tried on was made out of dark blue velvet, with a white lace Peter Pan collar and matching lace cuffs. The next one I tried was made out of pink chiffon, with puffy sleeves, a rounded necklines, and a pink satin sash at the waist. The first two dresses were definitely very nice, but when I put on the third dress, I knew it was perfect.

It was made out of this beautiful white fabric that the saleswoman said was called brocade. If you looked at it closely, you could see that there was actually a white design on a white background. The top fit snugly and had a really pretty curved neckline. But what I liked best of all were the little rows of white roses along the edges of the sleeves and neck and running down the back.

When I stepped out of the dressing room in it, both my mother and the saleswoman let out a sigh at the same time.

"Honey, you look beautiful," said my mother.

"That dress suits you wonderfully," agreed the saleswoman.

"I love it," I said happily.

"Okay," my mother told the saleswoman, "we'll take it. And a pair of shoes to match, please."

After the dress and shoes had been wrapped up and we were on our way back to the car, my mother said she wanted to stop at the pharmacy for a minute to pick up some things.

I followed my mother back to the cosmetics department, where she began looking for her favorite face cream.

"What's so special about that one?" I asked, helping her scan the shelves for it.

"Oh, it makes your skin feel wonderfully soft," said my mother. "There's nothing like it. I began using it years ago, and your father claims that my face is still as smooth as on the day we met." She smiled. "Oh, here it is," she said, reaching for a pink bottle on a high shelf. "I'll tell you what, let's get you some, too, Allison."

"Really, Mom?" I asked. "Do you think I'm

old enough to use face cream?"

"You're old enough, Al," she said. "It's probably time for you to start thinking about these things. In fact, maybe we should pick up a few more items for you while we're here."

"Like what?" I asked, taking the pink bottle of cream from her and looking it over.

"Well, for example, what are you using to condition your hair these days?"

I shrugged.

"I guess usually just whatever's in the bathroom when I wash my hair," I said.

"Come on," said my mother. "We'd better go up to the front of the store and get one of those plastic baskets to put our stuff in. We have quite a bit of shopping to do here."

By the time we were finished, my mother and I had filled an entire basket. In addition to the face cream, we had picked out a special shampoo and conditioner that was made just for long hair, a rose-scented bath oil, an avocado face mask, a manicure set with both clear and pale pink nail polish, two different shades of lip gloss, and even some mascara and blush to wear on special occasions.

While we were paying for it all, I suddenly

thought of something.

"Mom, now that I have all this stuff to use, do you think maybe I could get a mirror for my room?" I asked.

"Why, that's right," my mother said, a little surprised, "you don't have a mirror in there, do you? I guess it never really occurred to me before."

"It's just that it's kind of hard to get dressed and stuff if I can't see what I look like," I explained.

"Well, of course," said my mother. "A girl your age certainly needs a mirror." She thought a moment. "And I think I know just the one! There's a beautiful old oak-trimmed, full-length mirror down in the cellar, back at the house. Nooma brought it from the reservation when she and Grandpa first moved in. They never really had the space for it in their room at our house, so we've been storing it downstairs. I'm sure she'd love for you to use it."

"Thanks, Mom, it sounds perfect," I said, hugging her.

As we headed back to the car with my beauty supplies and my formal gown, I couldn't get over the feeling that no matter what ended up happening at the pageant, I was the luckiest girl in Acorn Falls.

Since it was Thursday, I decided to try to stay up late and listen to Lisa Lazure's Night Owl program. I was pretty curious, especially after all that stuff she had said to me during my interview about how people who have the chance to reach a lot of people also have a responsibility to spread important messages.

First I used my new avocado facial masque, and then I had a long, rose-scented bath. I had changed into my nightgown and was standing in front of the mirror that my father had brought up from the basement. I was putting on the face cream, when the Night Owl program began on WKZAP.

I sat down on my bed, propped up the pillows, and turned up the clock radio on my night stand.

"Good evening, everyone, this is Lisa Lazure, the Night Owl, staying with you all night," she began.

It was funny to hear her familiar voice coming over the radio. It was kind of exciting, too, because I almost felt like I knew her. She played a few slow songs, and I could feel myself getting a little sleepy. There was one song in particular that was really beautiful. I got comfortable and tried to listen to the words. I guess I must have fallen asleep while the song was playing, because when I woke up in the morning, the morning news was blaring. I switched it off and tried to remember the song. The tune was still clear in my head, and I even remembered a lot of the words.

Suddenly I had an idea. Maybe this was the song I should sing for the Talent competition of the pageant! Hadn't Randy said that all I needed was a song I really liked? But then I remembered — I didn't even know the name of the song or who had sung it. If only I had stayed awake long enough to hear Lisa Lazure announce it.

Then I thought of something. Randy would probably know! Randy's like a walking radio station; she knows more about current music than anyone I've ever met. I decided to ask her about it as soon as I got to school.

I found Randy by her locker.

"Hi, Al," she said, taking off her leather jacket and tossing it in her locker. "What's up?"

"Randy, I found a song to sing for the Talent competition of the pageant," I said excitedly.

"Great!" she said, her eyes lighting up. "What is it?'

"That's the problem," I told her. "I don't know. I heard it last night on the Night Owl program, but I fell asleep before Lisa Lazure announced the title or the singer. I remember some of it, though, and I thought maybe you would recognize it."

"Go ahead, songbird, let me hear it," she said.

I cleared my throat. I felt kind of funny singing in the hallway, with everyone at their lockers around me, but I really needed Randy's help.

"From a distance," I sang quietly, "the world looks blue and green, and the snow-capped mountains white . . ."

Randy's face lit up.

"Oh, sure," she said. "Nice choice, Al — that song won a Grammy for Song of the Year. It's called, 'From a Distance.'"

"Great, Randy! Thanks so much," I said happily.

"By the way, you sound great singing it," she said. "Listen, if you want me to pick up the sheet music for you, I'm heading down to the music store after school today to pick up some stuff for myself."

"Could you really, Randy?" I asked. "That would be perfect. I'm supposed to bring it with me to the next rehearsal."

"No problem," said Randy. "I'll give it to you at the meeting this afternoon."

"The meeting?" I asked, confused. "Oh, that's right, we have a S.A.F.E. meeting — I almost forgot."

I had been so busy thinking about the pageant, I had almost forgotten that the next recycling drive was on Monday, and that we still had to organize it.

After school the members of S.A.F.E. gathered in the empty classroom where we usually had our meetings. I was surprised because even more kids showed up — there must have been almost twenty kids in the room.

"All right, everyone," I began, "we have to plan the recycling drive for next Monday. Who wants to volunteer to stay after school then and sort?"

"I'll do it with you, Allison," Arizonna said eagerly. Arizonna's very concerned about the environment, and he's always willing to help out.

"Then I'll help you, too!" Billy Dixon said quickly. Billy's a really good friend of mine, and I think he's sometimes a little jealous of Arizonna.

"Great," I said. "I just want to remind everyone that you're going to have to do this on your own. I'm not going to be here Monday after school."

"But, Allison, you're S.A.F.E.'s founder," objected Sam, Sabrina's twin brother.

"Well, Sam," said Sabrina. "It just so happens that Allison and I have a very important rehearsal on Monday."

Sam smirked.

"Oh, you mean for your beauty pageant?" he said, making a face.

"I don't get it," said Billy. "I mean, what's to rehearse? Don't you just get all dressed up and walk around onstage?"

"No, Billy," I snapped suddenly. "It's a lot more than that." I looked around at them all. "You guys probably can't understand this, but being in a pageant is a lot of work."

"And it's not just about the way we look, you know," said Sabrina. "We each had to go through three interviews to get picked."

"And there's a Talent competition, too," Randy pointed out.

"Really!" huffed Sabrina. "I'd like to see you guys manage that!"

"I'm sorry about what I said, Allison," said Billy. "I guess I didn't know how much was involved."

"Yeah," said Sam. "We didn't mean anything. We were just teasing you."

"Are you really sorry, Sam?" asked Sabrina with a twinkle in her eye.

"I said I didn't mean it, Sabs!" he answered. "What do you want me to do?"

"I'm so glad you asked, Sam!" she said happily. "I know exactly what you should do — volunteer to help Arizonna and Billy at the recycling drive on Monday!"

Everyone laughed.

"All right, Sabs, you got me," said Sam, shaking his head. He looked at Billy and Arizonna. "Well, guys, I guess we'll be tying up, bagging, and wrapping about nine million bottles, cans, and newspapers on Monday, huh?"

Chapter Ten

"Can I borrow your hairbrush?" someone called out.

"Has anyone seen my tuba?" I heard another person ask frantically.

At last it was the night of the pageant, and all the contestants were rushing around the dressing room, getting ready. I still hadn't seen Sabs, but I was sure she was going to arrive any second.

Sure enough, Sabrina walked in a few seconds later, staggering under the weight of three huge garment bags.

"Sabs, what is all that?" I asked, rushing to help her with her load.

"Well," she said, flopping down into the nearest chair, "this one is my evening gown, and this one is my Juliet dress, and this one —" she paused, pointing to the largest of the three bags — "this one is Romeo!"

"What?" I said, amazed. "What are you talking about, Sabs?"

She grinned.

"For the balcony scene. Look," she said, unzipping a little of the garment bag and revealing a stuffed pillowcase with a hat on it. "I made him — isn't he great? He's wearing an old suit of my father's."

"But, Sabs," I said, "you can't act a scene opposite a bunch of old clothes and a pillow-case!"

"Don't worry," she said, "no one will be able to see his face. I'm going to prop him up against the side of the stage during my scene. That way, I can say both Romeo's and Juliet's lines. As long as I make my voice deeper and hide my face in my shawl or something when I say Romeo's part, no one will know!"

"Okay, cool," I said, shaking my head in amazement. "Hurry and get dressed in your sailor suit. The pageant's due to start soon."

Although it was almost half an hour later, it seemed like only a few minutes had passed when the lights went down, and we all crowd-ed around the door to the dressing room so we could get a glimpse of the stage. Jo Anne Phillips stood in the beam of a spotlight, waiting for the applause to die down.

"Welcome to the Junior Miss Acorn Falls Pageant," she began, flashing one of her perfect smiles. "The fifteen special girls you are about to meet were chosen from over five hundred original applicants. And once you all meet them, too, I'm sure you'll know why. But first I would like to introduce you to this evening's special guest, who will be crowning this year's Junior Miss Acorn Falls. She hails from our very own state of Minnesota, and it is my pleasure to welcome Miss America!"

Spotlights settled on Miss America, who had wavy black hair and was wearing a sequined white strapless evening gown. She stood up and waved.

"And now," said Jo Anne Phillips with a flourish, "please join me in welcoming our fifteen contestants!"

I turned to Sabrina and gave her a quick hug.

"Good luck, Sabs," I said.

"Thanks, Allison," she said, squeezing me back. "You too."

There was loud applause as we took our places on the stage. I could see the row of judges and Miss America in the very front of the audience, but behind them everything was in darkness. I wondered where my family was sitting.

Mrs. White took her place at the piano and began to play the opening chords of "Sing! Sing! Sing!" I took a deep breath and got ready.

Before I knew it, the song and dance routine was over, and we were all rushing back to the dressing room to change into our bathing suits.

"Wow," said Sabrina breathlessly, pulling on her royal blue one-piece. "That was great. They loved us! Did you hear all that applause?"

"It was fun," I agreed, adjusting my sash over my black bathing suit. I turned to Jeanine, who was pulling on her pink suit. "You were really good," I told her.

"Thanks," she said quietly. "Come on, we'd better hurry. They're starting."

One by one, we filed onstage as Jo Anne Phillips read our names out loud. When my turn came, I didn't miss a step, and I was really glad I had practiced walking before my mirror at home.

Next came the Talent competition, so I changed into the simple black skirt and cream-colored blouse I had decided to wear for my song.

The first person to perform was a girl with a long, red ponytail who played the tuba. She did pretty well and received a round of applause.

Next came Jeanine, who wore a long, lavender tutu and performed a complicated ballet routine in point shoes. The audience cheered loudly when she finished.

Next up was Sabs. As Jo Anne Phillips announced her name, I helped her pull Romeo out of his bag and adjust the curtain-shawl on her shoulders.

"Break a leg!" I whispered as she stepped out onstage.

When Sabrina crossed the stage and propped Romeo up against the wall, the audience began to giggle. At first I was really mad that the audience was laughing before Sabs even started. But then I realized something. Sabs was actually playing the scene as a comedy! When she recited Juliet's lines, she kept looking at Romeo with exasperation. When she said Romeo's lines, she made him sound more and more like he was falling asleep. By the end of the scene, the Romeo was on the floor, and the audience was in hysterics. It came as no surprise to me when they gave Sabrina a standing ovation.

"Sabs! You were fantastic!" I said, as she came backstage, dragging Romeo behind her.

"Thanks," she said breathlessly, her face glowing. "But one day, when I'm a truly great actress, I'll be onstage with a *real* Romeo!"

The next thing I knew, it was time for my song. Sabs gave my arm a squeeze as I smoothed my skirt and stepped out onstage.

I could hear my footsteps echoing as I walked across the stage. Just then someone coughed, and I felt my heart leap into my throat. I took a deep breath to calm myself and signaled Mrs. White that I was ready to begin.

As soon as I started to sing, I felt better. By the second line of the song my voice was coming out strong and clear. I remembered the image I had had of the earth as a perfect blue-green ball, and I relaxed completely. When I finished, the audience applauded loudly, and I knew I had done a good job.

Sabs was waiting to greet me backstage.

"That was great, Allison!" she said happily.

"Thanks, it was fun," I said. "Come on, let's

change quickly so we can watch the rest of the Talent competition."

I slipped my white brocade gown over my head and waited for Sabrina to button me up the back.

"You look beautiful, Allison," she said, adjusting the tiny white roses that ran down my back.

"So do you, Sabs. Your dress is perfect on you," I said. "Here, sit in the chair for just a minute. I think you need just a little more blush."

"Thanks," she answered, and hopped into the chair. When I finished, Sabrina turned toward the mirror and fluffed out one of the sleeves of her dark blue satin dress. "This dress almost makes me feel like becoming a professional pageant contestant, like Nicki, just to know I'd definitely get a chance to wear it again."

"Speaking of Nicki, she's onstage doing her Talent routine right now," I said. "Let's go watch."

We headed for the dressing room door and peeked out at the stage.

Nicki, who was wearing a red, white, and

blue sequined body suit and white patent-leather boots with tassels on them, was twirling a baton and marching around the stage to the tune of "Yankee Doodle Dandy."

"Pretty impressive, huh?" said Sabrina, as Nicki tossed the baton in the air and performed a cartwheel before catching it.

"The really incredible thing is the way she never stops smiling," I said, shaking my head as Nicki began tap-dancing and twirling her baton at the same time.

"No, the really incredible thing is that she's sort of a nice person," said Sabrina.

"I know," I said, watching Nicki slide into a split. "I guess this is just really important to her."

Suddenly I realized that no matter how this pageant turned out, I had learned a lot. I knew I would never be able to devote my life to this kind of thing, the way Nicki did, but I had also figured out that it was okay to care about your appearance, and to spend a little extra time on it now and then. I loved the way I felt in my evening gown, but it was nice to know I could go home and put on jeans later if I wanted to.

Finally it was time for the last part of the

pageant. We all lined up onstage in our gowns and waited. As Jo Anne Phillips called each of our names, we were supposed to stroll gracefully to the front of the stage and answer the question that one of the judges was going to ask us. It was one of the most nerve-racking parts of the pageant, because no one had any idea what the judges were going to ask.

The first name called was Christie French's. She walked carefully to the front of the stage in her long, peach-colored gown and waited for her question.

Arthur Lawrence, the owner of Dare, stood up in the judges' row and read Christie his question.

"Who has been the most influential person in your life, and why?" he asked.

Christie cleared her throat.

"The most influential person in my life has been my mother," she said. "Because she has taught me what it means to be a successful woman."

It seemed like a good answer to me. The audience applauded, and Christie returned to the row of contestants at the back of the stage.

The next person called was Jeanine. Roberta

Andrews from Limelight Cosmetics asked her what she would wish for if she could have one wish. Jeanine answered that she would wish for every child in the world to have enough to eat, a place to sleep, and someone to love them.

After a couple more contestants, Jo Anne Phillips called Sabrina's name. I watched proudly as Sabrina walked easily across the stage in her blue gown. She didn't look nervous at all.

Sabrina's question was from Mike Kinney, the former hockey player.

"What would you say is your greatest asset?" he asked.

Sabrina smiled.

"I think my greatest asset is probably my sense of humor," she answered. "It helps me when I meet new people, it helps me stay cheerful, and it's even helped me out of a few tough spots."

The audience laughed, probably thinking of Sabrina's scene in the Talent competition. They applauded as she walked back and took her place again.

"And now," said Jo Anne Phillips, "our next contestant, Contestant Number 11, is Veronica

Lane Callahan."

Nicki glided to the front of the stage in her powder-blue chiffon gown.

Lisa Lazure stood up to ask her question.

"What do you think is the most important thing the new Junior Miss Acorn Falls will be able to accomplish?" she asked.

I had to admit I was a little disappointed. I would have liked to get that question. It was all about exactly what Lisa Lazure and I had talked about in our interview.

Right away, Nicki went into a long speech about how the new Junior Miss Acorn Falls would be a role model to other kids her age. She went on to talk about her work at a soup kitchen for the homeless, the arts and crafts program she helped out with at a local children's home, and the time she spent at the local animal shelter. She said it would be the biggest honor and the greatest responsibility of her life if she was to be crowned Junior Miss Acorn Falls. By the time she was done, I was sure the whole audience was in love with her.

Next came my turn. I walked to the front of the stage as Jo Anne Phillips read my name.

It turned out that my question was from Mr.

Hansen.

He stood up and smiled at me.

"There's been a lot of discussion of Community Service throughout this pageant procedure," Mr. Hansen read. "I'd like to know what the word *community* means to you."

"Well," I began, "community can be as small as your school, or as big as the planet. I think it's very important to remember that we are all members of the world community, and that we all have a responsibility to the earth. The best way for each of us to really make a difference, though, is at our own local community level. People my age can start in their own schools, by starting recycling drives, for example. As the saying goes — 'Think globally, act locally.'"

I thought I had answered pretty well, but as I returned to my spot to the sound of the audience's applause, all I could think about was how happy I was that it was all finally over. Now all we had to do was wait for the judges' decision.

A few moments later, Jo Anne Phillips held the envelope in her hand.

"All right, ladies and gentlemen," she said, flashing a smile. "This is the moment you have all been waiting for." She tore open the envelope. "The first award I am going to announce is for the title of Miss Congeniality. This award goes to the girl the judges feel has shown outstanding spirit and a lively personality." She paused. "And the award for Miss Congeniality goes to — Contestant Number 8, Sabrina Wells!"

For a minute, Sabrina looked like she was about to faint. She just stood there with her mouth hanging open. Finally the two girls next to her gave her a push, and she stumbled toward the front of the stage. By the time Jo Anne Phillips had handed her a bouquet of roses, tears were streaming down Sabrina's cheeks.

"Thank you, thank you!" she called, blowing kisses to the audience. I thought she might even be about to make a speech, but Jo Anne Phillips gave her a look, and after a few more kisses, Sabrina made it back to her place in line.

I sneaked a peek down the line at her and gave her the thumbs-up sign to congratulate her.

"And now I will read the names of the second runner-up, the first runner-up, and finally, the name of the new Junior Miss Acorn Falls," Jo Anne Phillips was saying.

Suddenly everything was quiet. It was like the whole audience was holding its breath.

"Our second runner-up," Jo Anne Phillips announced, "is Contestant Number 12, Allison Cloud!"

Before I realized exactly what was happening, everyone was hugging me. I made my way to the front of the stage and accepted the flowers that Jo Anne Phillips handed me.

"And the first runner-up is Contestant Number 1, Jeanine Jones!" Jo Anne Phillips announced.

I smiled at Jeanine as she stood next to me and accepted her flowers.

"And now," said Jo Anne Phillips dramatically, "the name we're all waiting to hear. The new Junior Miss Acorn Falls is — Contestant Number 11, Veronica Lane Callahan!"

I wasn't exactly surprised. After all, Nicki had made a career out of entering pageants. Of course, I was a little disappointed not to have won, but I was also pretty proud that I had been named one of the finalists.

"Congratulations," I said to Nicki as Miss America stepped on the stage to put the crown on her head.

From that moment on, it seemed like all I did was get hugged by people. First all the contestants hugged each other. Then Sabs and I gave each other a special huge hug.

As soon as I got backstage, I was surrounded by people.

My father handed me a huge bouquet of red roses.

"I figured you deserved the rest of the bush," he joked.

"Oh, honey, we're so proud of you," my mother said, throwing her arms around me.

"That's our little girl!" said my grandfather, beaming.

"You did a lovely job with the song," added Nooma.

Charlie, who was riding piggyback on Mary, handed me a piece of drawing paper covered with lopsided hearts.

"That's for you, Allie, for being good in the contest," he told me.

"Congratulations, Allison," said Mary, smiling.

Just then I saw Mr. Hansen making his way through the crowd.

"Congratulations, my dear," he said, shaking my hand heartily. "I was very impressed with the way you answered my question about community."

"Thank you, Mr. Hansen," I said.

"Oh, one of the other judges asked me to give you this," he said, handing me a piece of paper.

It was a note from Lisa Lazure, inviting me to come on her radio program to talk about S.A.F.E.!

"Thanks, Mr. Hansen, this is great!" I said happily.

"Oh, yes, and by the way," he said, "I've been doing some thinking about those recycling drives of yours, and I'd like to devote a school assembly to the topic, if you'd like to organize it. You know, sort of spread the word around that Bradley needs to do its part, too."

"I'd love to," I told him.

Then I saw Randy and Katie making their way toward me, with Sabrina between them.

"Congratulations, Al!" said Randy, high-fiving me so hard my hand stung.

"You guys were great," gushed Katie.

"Well, Allison, we did it!" said Sabrina happily.

"I know!" I answered. "And guess what? Lisa Lazure invited me to come on her radio program to talk about S.A.F.E."

"Cool!" said Randy.

"That's great," agreed Katie. "That way you can spread the S.A.F.E. message after all!"

"And that's not all," I told them. "Mr. Hansen's going to let me organize a school assembly about recycling."

"That'll definitely bring in more cans and bottles," said Katie.

"Hey, I just thought of something new to recycle," said Sabrina.

"What?" I asked her.

"Evening gowns," she joked. "We can make them into miniskirts, shawls, even pants, and sell them to next year's pageant contestants to raise money for S.A.F.E.!"

"Oh, Sabrina!" I laughed. "I've got the best friends in the world!"

TALK BACK!
TELL US WHAT YOU THINK ABOUT GIRL TALK BOOKS

Name _____

Address _____

City _____ State _____ Zip _____

Birth Day _____ Mo._____ Year _____

Telephone Number (____)_____

1) Did you like this GIRL TALK book?

Check one: YES_____ NO_____

2) Would you buy another Girl Talk book?

Check one: YES_____ NO_____

If you like GIRL TALK books, please answer questions 3-5;
otherwise go directly to question 6

3) What do you like most about GIRL TALK books?

Check one: Characters_____ Situations_____
            Telephone Talk_____Other_____.

4) Who is your favorite GIRL TALK character?

Check one: Sabrina_____ Katie_____ Randy_____
Allison_____ Stacy_____ Other (give name) _____

5) Who is your *least* favorite character?

_____

6) Where did you buy this GIRL TALK book?

Check one: Book store____Toy store____Discount store____
Grocery store____Supermarket____Other (give name)_____

Please turn over to continue survey.

7) How many GIRL TALK books have you read?
Check one: 0_____   1 to 2_____   3 to 4 _____   5 or more_____

8) In what type of store would you look for GIRL TALK books?
Book store_____Toy store_____Discount store_____
Grocery store_____Supermarket_____Other (give name)_____

9) Which type of store you would visit most often if you wanted to buy a GIRL TALK book.
Check *only* one: Book store_____Toy store_____
Discount store_____Grocery store_____Supermarket_____
Other (give name)_____

10) How many books do you read in a month?
Check one: 0_____   1 to 2_____   3 to 4 _____   5 or more_____

11) Do you read any of these books?
Check those you have read:
The Babysitters Club_____   Nancy Drew_____
Pen Pals_____   Sweet Valley High _____
Sweet Valley Twins_____Gymnasts_____

12) Where do you shop most often to buy these books?
Check one: Book store_____Toy store_____
Discount store_____Grocery store_____Supermarket_____
Other (give name)_____

13) What other kinds of books do you read most often?
_____

14) What would you like to read more about in GIRL TALK?
_____
_____

Send completed form to :
GIRL TALK Survey # 3 Western Publishing Company, Inc.
1220 Mound Avenue, Mail Station #85
Racine, Wisconsin 53404

**LOOK FOR THE AWESOME GIRL TALK BOOKS
IN A STORE NEAR YOU!**

Fiction
  #1 WELCOME TO JUNIOR HIGH!
  #2 FACE-OFF!
  #3 THE NEW YOU
  #4 REBEL, REBEL
  #5 IT'S ALL IN THE STARS
  #6 THE GHOST OF EAGLE MOUNTAIN
  #7 ODD COUPLE
  #8 STEALING THE SHOW
  #9 PEER PRESSURE
  #10 FALLING IN LIKE
  #11 MIXED FEELINGS
  #12 DRUMMER GIRL
  #13 THE WINNING TEAM
  #14 EARTH ALERT!
  #15 ON THE AIR
  #16 HERE COMES THE BRIDE
  #17 STAR QUALITY
  #18 KEEPING THE BEAT
  #19 FAMILY AFFAIR
  #20 ROCKIN' CLASS TRIP
  #21 BABY TALK
  #22 PROBLEM DAD
  #23 HOUSE PARTY
  #24 COUSINS
  #25 HORSE FEVER
  #26 BEAUTY QUEENS

Chapter One

"Katie, this pizzaburger is great!" exclaimed my best friend, Sabrina Wells. She licked some tomato sauce off her lip and continued to devour the messy burger.

"Whoa, Sabs!" said Randy Zak, another one of my friends. "You're acting like you haven't eaten in days!" Randy was dressed in a black babydoll dress with big buttons in front, red-and-black plaid tights, and her favorite black granny boots. I guess I don't have to tell you that black is her favorite color. Even her hair is black.

Randy reached for a french fry covered in cat-sup from the plateful of them that she was shar-ing with me and our other best friend, Allison Cloud. I'm Katie Campbell, and I was sitting with my friends at a booth in Fitzie's Soda Shoppe after school on Wednesday. Fitzie's is only a few blocks from Bradley Junior High, where we're all in seventh grade. As usual,

1

Fitzie's was pretty crowded, because tons of kids from Bradley come here after school.

"I feel like I haven't eaten in a week!" Sabs said, brushing back her curly red hair so that she wouldn't get pizza sauce on it. "I mean, I couldn't eat any breakfast this morning or I would have been late for school."

"Oh, well, that's a change!" Randy joked. She looked across the booth at me and Al, and the three of us started giggling.

The truth is, Sabs is late for school almost every day. But I guess having to share one bathroom with three brothers every morning would make anyone late for school. I mean, I have a hard time getting ready for school and I only have to share a bathroom with my new stepbrother, Michel.

Sabs was so caught up in what she was saying that she didn't even seem to hear Randy's comment. "And then that lunch at school today!" she continued, making a face. "Yuck! What was it anyway?"